WALK-OFF

ALSO BY DEREK JETER

WALK-OFF

DEREK JETER

with Paul Mantell

SIMON & SCHUSTER BOOKS FOR YOUNG READERS

New York   London   Toronto   Sydney   New Delhi

SIMON & SCHUSTER BOOKS FOR YOUNG READERS
An imprint of Simon & Schuster Children's Publishing Division
1230 Avenue of the Americas, New York, New York 10020

SIMON & SCHUSTER BOOKS FOR YOUNG READERS
and related marks are trademarks of Simon & Schuster, Inc.
For information about special discounts for bulk purchases, please contact Simon & Schuster Special Sales at 1-866-506-1949 or business@simonandschuster.com.
The Simon & Schuster Speakers Bureau can bring authors to your live event. For more information or to book an event, contact the Simon & Schuster Speakers Bureau at 1-866-248-3049 or visit our website at www.simonspeakers.com.
Interior design by Krista Vossen
The text for this book was set in Centennial.
Manufactured in the United States of America
0323 FFG
First Edition
2 4 6 8 10 9 7 5 3 1
CIP data for this book is available from the Library of Congress.
ISBN 9781665931212
ISBN 9781665931236 (ebook)

Thank you to all of the readers of every age who have been on this journey with me throughout the series. Wishing you all the best in how your own stories unfold.

A Note About the Text

The rules of Little League followed in this book are the rules of the present day. There are six innings in each game. Every player on a Little League baseball team must play at least two innings of every game in the field and have at least one at bat. In any given contest, there is a limit on the number of pitches a pitcher can throw, in accordance with age. Pitchers who are eight years old are allowed a maximum of fifty pitches in a game, pitchers who are nine or ten years old are allowed seventy-five pitches per game, and pitchers who are eleven or twelve years old are allowed eighty-five pitches.

Dear Reader,

Walk-Off is inspired by some of my experiences growing up. The book portrays the values my parents instilled in me and the lessons they have taught me about how to remain true to myself and embrace the unique differences in everyone around me.

Walk-Off is based on the lesson that life is a daily challenge. I hope readers recognize that every challenge is an opportunity for growth and that working hard to achieve goals brings the greatest fulfillment. Those are principles I have lived by in order to achieve my dreams. I hope you enjoy reading!

Derek Jeter

DEREK JETER'S 10 LIFE LESSONS

1. Set Your Goals High (*The Contract*)

2. Think Before You Act (*Hit & Miss*)

3. Deal with Growing Pains (*Change Up*)

4. The World Isn't Always Fair (*Fair Ball*)

5. Find the Right Role Models (*Curveball*)

6. Don't Be Afraid to Fail (*Fast Break*)

7. Have a Strong Supporting Cast
   (*Strike Zone*)

8. Be Serious but Have Fun (*Wind Up*)

9. Be a Leader, Follow the Leader
   (*Switch-Hitter*)

10. Life Is a Daily Challenge (*Walk-Off*)

CONTRACT FOR DEREK JETER

1. Family Comes First. Attend our nightly dinner.
2. Be a Role Model for Sharlee. (She looks to you to model good behavior.)
3. Do Your Schoolwork and Maintain Good Grades (As or Bs).
4. Bedtime. Lights out at nine p.m. on school nights.
5. Do Your Chores. Take out the garbage, clean your room on weekends, and help with the dishes.
6. Respect Others. Be a good friend, classmate, and teammate. Listen to your teachers, coaches, and other adults.
7. Respect Yourself. Take good care of your body and your mind. Avoid alcohol and drugs. Surround yourself with positive friends with strong values.
8. Work Hard. You owe it to yourself and those around you to give your all. Do your best in everything that you do.
9. Think Before You Act.

Failure to comply will result in the loss of playing sports and hanging out with friends. Extra-special rewards include attending a Major League Baseball game, choosing a location for dinner, and selecting another event of your choice.

CONTENTS

CONTENTS

Chapter One

NEW BEGINNINGS

"That ball was outside!" Derek Jeter sprang up from his seat on the living room couch, his arms outstretched in protest. "Dad, that ump needs glasses."

"Now, Derek, that was a borderline pitch," Mr. Jeter replied, gazing at the TV screen as the dejected Tigers batter headed back to the dugout. "Give the umps a little slack. It's a hard job."

"I think the hitter should have swung," said Derek's little sister, Sharlee. Over the winter she'd become obsessed with baseball, and hitting in particular, mostly because their dad had started taking her along when he and Derek went to the indoor batting cages to practice.

"Who was that batter, anyway? I never saw him before," Derek said.

"Jim Faye," said Mr. Jeter. "He was in the minors last year."

"There are so many new guys on the team," Derek complained, sinking back down into his seat. "I barely know who's who now. Where are all the guys from last year?"

"Well, they traded some away, let others go to free agency. The Tigers are rebuilding, Derek."

"Why? They had a great team a couple of seasons ago."

"Well, things change, Son. It's a new season. New players, and a nice clean slate, too. Everyone's in first place on opening day. Speaking of which, are you two excited for your leagues to start up next weekend?"

"Yes!" Sharlee exulted, bouncing up and down in her chair. "I can't wait. I'm going to hit a home run every game this year!"

"She does have a mean swing," Mr. Jeter said, glancing at Derek with a wink.

Derek laughed. "Hey, I'm just glad to get on the field again after all this time. It feels like years."

Derek really was feeling jazzed about the new season. First and foremost he was now on the travel team. And unlike last fall, when practically all they'd done was practice, this spring would bring a whole slew of games against the stiffest competition in the region.

It made Derek feel like he was an elite player—at least in Kalamazoo. Of course, his dreams were much bigger.

He wanted to be the best, not just in Kalamazoo but in the whole country.

On top of travel baseball, Derek would also be playing his final season in Junior League. Next year, in eighth grade, he'd move up to the Senior League, where the players were older, bigger, taller, faster, and stronger.

Derek himself had grown four inches over the past winter. If he kept it up, he might even get to be six feet tall, which would be really cool. Onward and upward, that was how he looked at it. Every day brought a new challenge, and he would work as hard as necessary to be ready.

"Derek!" his mom called from the kitchen. "Sharlee! Anyone going to clean up in here?"

Derek and Sharlee hopped up and went to help. Their chores around the house were all laid out in the contracts they'd signed with their parents. In exchange for privileges, they had clear responsibilities, and doing dishes after meals was one of them.

"There are so many leftovers," Sharlee complained as she and Derek packed them up for later.

"Easter Sunday lunch," their mom remarked, shrugging. "Should I have just made peanut butter sandwiches?"

"No!" Derek and Sharlee said at once, and they all laughed. Their mom had made a heaping feast, and Derek couldn't imagine eating again till at least Tuesday.

"You guys ready to go back to school tomorrow?" Mrs. Jeter asked.

"Yes!" said Derek.

"No," said Sharlee at the same time.

"What's wrong?" Derek asked his sister. "You just had ten days off, didn't you?"

"But it's springtime," Sharlee explained. "Finally. I want to be outside. Why can't we have classes out on the lawn?"

"When you're in charge of the schools, you can make those decisions," Mrs. Jeter said, patting Sharlee on the shoulder. "And don't forget to dry the frying pan."

Sharlee moaned, but did as she was told.

Derek had had the same ten days off, but Sharlee had been hanging out with her friends the whole time. Ciara had been at their house almost every day over the break, and so had the Parker triplets—London, Adriana, and Abby. They'd driven Derek crazy with their talking and laughing and playing all kinds of games he wasn't interested in.

His own best friend, Vijay, had been away with his parents, visiting family in India the whole time. Derek's other best friend, Dave, had moved to Hong Kong with his parents the year before. His friend Avery, who lived across town, had gone traveling with her mom over Easter week, so Derek had spent a lot of time alone, getting a head start on reading assignments for school.

Last term he'd fallen behind in his schoolwork while playing both basketball and baseball. He'd done fine on his final grades, but not without a lot of hard work cramming at the last minute. He was determined to get ahead of the game this time around, because playing in two baseball leagues at once was going to eat up a lot of time between now and the end of June.

"Can I go over to the Hill?" Derek asked his mom. "I think Vijay might be home by now."

"Sure," said his mom. "Give him my best. Be back by six, okay?"

"We're actually eating *supper* tonight? After *that lunch? Seriously?*"

"You're a growing boy, old man," his mom said with a wry smile. "You're full now, but you've been basically a bottomless pit the last six months."

He could tell she was happy that he'd gotten taller. For the longest time it had seemed like every other kid but him was growing into a man. Now he'd joined the party.

On the other hand, in a couple of months he'd be an actual teenager. The thought of it made him uncomfortable, and a little sad. Why did things always have to change? Why couldn't life stay like it had been his whole life?

Vijay was already out on Jeter's Hill (named for Derek because he spent almost every free minute there, playing ball). Vijay was playing catch with Harry Hicks, who also lived at Mount Royal Townhouses and whom Derek had known since he was a little kid.

Derek had never been happier to see his best buddy. They exchanged hugs and high fives with their mitts, and their elaborate secret handshake with their throwing hands.

Harry came over to greet him. "Hey, Jeter," he said.

"How was Disneyland?" Derek asked him. Harry and his family had just returned from the West Coast, he knew.

"Awesome, but I might have outgrown some of the stuff," Harry admitted. "My little sister went crazy for it, though."

"So would mine," Derek said, thinking of Sharlee and remembering how excited she'd gotten at that water park in New Jersey last summer.

"Hey, are you on the Yankees this season?" Harry asked him.

"No," said Derek. "The Reds."

"Bummer," said Harry. "Hey, I've got to go. My grandma's coming over this afternoon. See you guys in school." Harry took off at a trot, checking his wristwatch.

"How about you, Vij? What team are you on?"

"Oh . . . me?" Vijay had a funny look on his face, almost like he was suddenly shy.

"You see anyone else here?"

"Um, I'm not playing ball this year," Vijay said softly, looking away.

"Say *what*?" Derek couldn't believe his ears. "But . . . we've been on the same team every year since . . ."

"Since the beginning," Vijay said, nodding. "But for every beginning there's an end."

"You mean you're not going to play ball again? Ever?"

"Well, like, here on the Hill, of course I'll still play. But I'm just . . . I don't know. . . ."

Derek wanted to press the issue—to ask Vijay why. He just couldn't understand.

Vijay had improved greatly over his years in Little League. He'd started as a complete novice and had wound up being an asset to the team. But he'd never been one of the better players. And while many of the kids had started their growth spurts already, Vijay hadn't grown much at all the past year or so. He still looked for all the world like a fifth grader.

"Remember that kid last spring, who got his arm broken by a fastball?" Vijay reminded Derek.

Derek nodded. "He wasn't on our team, but we all signed his cast anyway."

"I'll bet he's not playing ball anymore either. I wouldn't want to get hit like that. Some of the pitchers are six feet tall!"

It suddenly hit Derek that Vijay was really quitting the game. "Gee," he said, feeling suddenly emotional. "It won't be the same without you."

"You'll do fine," Vijay assured him. "You've got what it takes, Derek. You always have, and you keep getting better every year. I've kind of hit my ceiling, if you know what I mean."

Derek wanted to argue with him further, but Vijay preempted him. "Anyway, don't feel bad on my account. I've got a new passion."

"Oh yeah? What?"

"Are you ready?" Vijay asked, as if he were about to reveal the secret of the universe. Spreading his hands out and smiling blissfully, he said, "Video games!"

"Video games?" Derek repeated, confused.

"Derek, it's a whole new world. No, a whole new *universe.* Wait till you try them."

"I've tried them," Derek said. "A couple of times. I think it was over at Jeff Jacobson's house. *Super Something Brothers.* . . . It was pretty fun."

"*Super MARIO Brothers,*" Vijay corrected him. "And now I have my own game console at home."

"Wow, really?"

"My parents got it for me for my birthday, right before we left for India. I took it with me, and I was playing it half the time there. My parents even yelled at me because I was ignoring my cousins to play it. But, Derek, you can't believe how much fun it is!"

"Well, next time I'm over at your house . . ."

"*Totally.* And guess what? Now there's actually a real video game store in town, where you can go and play all these games on gigantic screens, and you can win tickets to redeem for prizes, and you can blow your entire allowance in one afternoon of supreme ecstasy!"

Derek had to laugh. He knew Vijay was joking, but he also knew that his friend meant every word. Vijay had already probably blown an insane amount of chore money at the new arcade.

Derek had seen the place from the outside—it was right across the street from the batting cages—but he'd never been inside. He couldn't imagine having time for video games.

After playing catch with Vijay, Derek walked home feeling dejected. He'd been so excited about playing in two leagues, one with old friends and the other with new ones. But without his best pal, Little League baseball wouldn't be what he had envisioned.

Last fall he'd worn himself out playing basketball and baseball at the same time. In fact, he'd wound up getting hurt and missing substantial chunks of the season.

Maybe I should just do travel team, he thought. Multiple games a week for the next two months was a lot, for sure. And travel back and forth ate up a lot of time too.

On the other hand, the more baseball he played, the better he would get—right? Derek was confident he could handle it, and also get his schoolwork done.

But it just wouldn't be the same without Vijay.

Chapter Two
ALL SHOOK UP

"Your attention, class."

Derek quickly stopped talking to Gary Parnell and turned around to face front. Every other kid did the same. When Mr. Laithwaite called for attention, he got it.

"I know you're all still buzzing with excitement from your spring vacations and want to tell each other all about it. But let me remind you that school is now back in session, and we have lots of work to do before we begin finals prep."

Derek winced. When Mr. Laithwaite called for the class's attention, it was rarely good news.

Derek had already begun thinking about finals, even though they were still six weeks away. He knew you could never do enough reviewing, and with so much time about to be eaten up by baseball, there'd be little time to study.

"I'm going to task you all with one more substantial project over the next month," Mr. Laithwaite said, writing the word "ADDICTION" on the blackboard.

"You're all going to be teenagers soon, if you aren't already. As I'm sure you know, that presents a set of new and difficult challenges. Every day you will have to navigate a stormy sea of temptations, dangers, and disappointments.

"Ultimately you will chart your own course to adulthood, but I hope this assignment will give you a head start in defending yourselves against one of the chief dangers: addiction."

He pointed to the big letters on the blackboard for emphasis. "This is your chance to educate yourselves beforehand. Forewarned is forearmed, as they say." He looked around the classroom, catching every student's glance in turn.

"Each of you will write a six-page paper, not including research citations, detailing every aspect of a particular addiction. You'll have to visit the public library, as well as our own here at school, and do lots of reading on your topic, and on addiction in general. You will have four weeks to hand in your work. Questions?"

A murmur went through the room. Derek felt a shiver go up and down his spine. His parents had always warned him about addictions. In fact, his dad was a drug and alcohol abuse counselor. Mr. Jeter always kept his clients' personal stories private, but he often spoke of the horrors that addiction can inflict on a person.

But that was not what had made Derek shiver. It was the prospect of all that extra work, suddenly thrust upon him out of nowhere. How was he going to have time to fit it all in and still study for finals while playing baseball in two leagues at once?

On Mondays, Derek's mom always worked till six o'clock, because there was always extra work that had piled up over the weekend that had to be handled right away.

So Monday was Mr. Jeter's day to prepare dinner. Because he worked at the university in town seeing student clients, his schedule was more flexible.

Derek and Sharlee were setting the table. "My teacher gives us so much work," she was complaining. "Three whole sheets of examples, just in math!"

"You think that's a lot?" Derek shot back. "Wait till you get to seventh grade. You have no idea."

"Hmph," said Sharlee, crossing her arms and scowling. "If you have so much work, how come you're playing in two leagues when I only get to be in one?"

Derek made a face. Sharlee had a way of always putting her finger right on the sore spot. "It's just different," he told her. "You'll see when you're older."

"Work is good for you," said their father, who had evidently been listening while standing at the stove. "It helps you grow up right, and it keeps you on the straight path. Develops your character. Remember, nothing worth having comes easy, and you shouldn't want it to. You should want to work hard for what you earn."

Derek and Sharlee looked at each other, and Sharlee rolled her eyes, making Derek laugh.

"You think I'm kidding?" Mr. Jeter asked.

"No, Dad," Derek said. "Sorry. Sharlee made me laugh."

"Hey," Sharlee said. "Don't blame me. You cracked up on your own."

"Okay, okay," said their dad. "Dinner is ready. Sit yourselves down. Mom will be here any minute." He glanced at the clock on the wall. "In fact, she's overdue."

And just then the front door opened and Mrs. Jeter burst into the house. She looked excited and was wearing a big, broad smile. "Hello, everybody! How was your day?"

"Good."

"Fine."

They all replied at once.

"Well, ask me how my day was," she told them.

"How was it?" Derek and Sharlee said.

"It was *super*," said Mrs. Jeter. "I finally got my raise!"

"You did? Hooray!" said Mr. Jeter, taking her in his arms and giving her a big hug.

"Yay, Mommy!" Sharlee cried.

"That's great, Mom!" Derek said, getting up and hugging her in turn.

Mrs. Jeter beamed. "And it came with a promotion, no less!"

"Wow! That's fantastic, Dot," said Mr. Jeter, taking her briefcase and setting it on a chair out of the way. "Come sit down and tell us all about it. Dinner's just ready."

"Thanks, Jeter," she said, sitting down between Derek and Sharlee. "Well. It sure smells good."

"Thank you, thank you," said the chef, taking a seat himself. "Dig in, everyone."

Derek had lost count of all the times his mom and dad had been worried about money. Now they'd have some breathing room, and even be able to put some funds aside for a rainy day—or for his and Sharlee's college down the road. . . .

And then he heard his father say some words that froze him to his chair:

"You know, Dot, now that we're going to be more secure, maybe it's time for us to think about moving to a house."

WHAT? Weren't they in their own house right now?

"But, Dad—" Derek began.

But his dad wasn't finished. "You'll be turning thirteen in a couple of months," he told Derek. "And just look how tall Sharlee's getting." Sharlee beamed with pride at the compliment. "It's time you each had a decent-size bedroom. It'll be good to have a bigger place.

"Maybe even a house with a backyard where you two can

run around and play catch," Mrs. Jeter chimed in excitedly.

"Can we have a swimming pool in the backyard?" Sharlee asked, her eyes getting wide with anticipation.

"Well, maybe we can have a kiddie pool," Mr. Jeter said. "That's more than we can do here."

Derek sat there, as still as a stone. "I'm not moving," he said.

"Derek!" his mom chided him. "What's wrong? Wouldn't you like a bigger bedroom? A backyard?"

"I like it right here," Derek said, feeling his eyes well up. He blinked furiously, forcing the tears back where they'd come from, pressing his lips firmly together to try to stop the tidal wave that was crashing over him.

"Oh, honey," said his mom, coming over and hugging him. "I know you love it here at Mount Royal. *Of course* you hate the idea of leaving. But think where we'll be *going*."

"It won't be so far away," his dad assured him. "You'll still have all your old friends, and you can always come and visit."

Yeah, right, thought Derek skeptically. He knew how that usually turned out. Dave had moved to Hong Kong the year before, and all that was left of that friendship were occasional letters.

"We'll still be in Kalamazoo," his dad assured him. "After all, your mom and I both work here. We're not leaving town."

"It's not the end of the world, old man," said his mom. "You'll see. We'll find a great house, and you'll fall in love with it."

Derek didn't think so. Up till now he'd never thought about how much he loved where he lived. But now he felt it strongly—like a stabbing pain of loss.

Just the thought of moving all the way across town, where he'd have to get a lift from his parents every time he wanted to see his friends: Isaiah, Harry, Jeff . . . and especially Vijay.

Just when he'd been looking forward to spring too. Now Vijay wasn't going to be on his team, and by the time summer rolled around, Derek might be torn away from everything he'd always loved.

Why does everything have to change? he lamented silently. *Why can't things just stay the same?*

Chapter Three
THE NEXT LEVEL

When he got to travel team practice, Derek was taken aback by Coach Russell's greeting.

"Wow! Is that you, Derek?"

"Yeah, it's me," was all he could think of in reply.

"Amazing. You're like a different kid. How many inches have you grown since last fall?"

Derek knew the answer to that one. "Six. Four since Christmas."

He was thrilled that Coach Russell had noticed. Until late fall Derek had been average height for his age, just skinnier than most kids.

Coach shook his head in wonder. "Well, you keep it up long enough, I'll have to try you at third base. You'll be too tall to be a shortstop."

A sudden wave of panic washed over Derek at the dreadful thought. But Coach nipped it in the bud. "Just kidding," he said, clapping Derek on the shoulder. "How tall is Cal Ripken, right?"

Derek knew that one too. "Six feet, four inches."

"So quit worrying," Coach said. "Until you hit the big six-oh, at least. Which, at the rate you're going, won't be too long."

Derek's face took on that worried look again.

"Hey!" Coach said. "*Kidding!* Okay?"

Derek blew out a breath and tried to let go of the lingering image of growing too tall to play shortstop for the Yankees.

"Seriously, though," Coach went on, unpacking the duffel bag full of bats and batting helmets, "I want to try everyone in multiple positions this season—at least for the first few games. So don't be disappointed if you find yourself somewhere else early on."

"But, Coach—" Derek started to say.

"This is about the *whole team*, not just you," Coach Russell explained, cutting him off. "I want you kids to learn what it's like all around the diamond. You never know. We might find some new perfect fits. At the very least you'll each improve your skill sets."

And that was the end of the discussion. Coach Russell went on to greet several other players who'd shown up while he'd been talking to Derek.

Derek did play all over the infield at that first practice. He actually made a spectacular leaping catch while playing first, a catch he couldn't have made back in the fall, when he'd been six inches shorter.

He also stood out at the plate, hitting hard shot after hard shot, to all fields. He even showed off his bunting skills.

And when it came to baserunning, with his longer legs taking bigger strides, Derek's speed had increased significantly.

"Impressive," Coach said as he hit the button on his stopwatch and read the result. "Four seconds faster than last year."

Derek flushed with pride, although getting taller hadn't taken any work at all on his part. Still, he'd been diligent about going to the batting cages all winter. Plus he'd started jogging to places instead of walking, just to build up his stamina and work up a sweat.

And now he was seeing the results. By the end of practice he was back at shortstop, feeling right at home on this team of serious ballplayers, all of whom were capable of helping the team win.

He couldn't wait until their first game.

At the end of practice, Coach Russell gathered the whole team together and handed out season schedules.

Derek took a quick look at his. The team had games on Saturdays and Wednesday afternoons, with occasional practices sprinkled in on other weekday early evenings.

Seeing the schedule on paper, laid out calendar-style, Derek suddenly realized he was going to be missing a lot of Little League games because of scheduling conflicts with the travel team—especially on Saturdays.

Derek felt like a balloon that someone had let all the air out of. This was his last year in Junior League, after all, and he'd wanted to go out on a high note. Showing up for only half the games did not qualify.

On the other hand, he had to look at things realistically. With travel team on top of Little League, he'd be playing ball at least twice a week, and sometimes three times, if you threw in practices and weekday games.

There was no way he could have played in every game anyway, he told himself.

Looking at the schedule also made it crystal clear that it was going to be a challenge to find time for everything else—including his term paper and studying for finals. Derek folded the paper and slipped it into the back pocket of his jeans. He jogged to the curb, where his mom was in the car waiting to pick him up and drive him home.

"How'd it go, old man?" she asked as he got in and buckled up.

"Fine."

"Just fine? Not stupendous?"

"Seriously, Mom. It went well. I hit okay. I made good catches. Can we talk about something else now?"

"Oh boy. Something's on your mind. I can see that. Want to talk about it?"

"Not really. Maybe some other time."

"Well, okay. Anytime. I'm all ears."

Derek sat silently the rest of the way home. A couple of times he took out the schedule and looked at it again, mentally filling the empty spaces with Little League games and study times. There wasn't a lot of empty space left over—for things like *friends*, for instance.

The next time Derek saw Vijay, outside of Mr. Laithwaite's classroom, that is, was five days later, on Friday afternoon in the school library.

Derek had been putting off doing research for his paper, but he knew he had to get started and at least find some material on addictions before the other kids in his class checked all the relevant books out of the library.

There was Vijay, looking through the shelves, which didn't surprise Derek. Vijay had always been a brainiac, good at every subject. Only when it came to sports did he need help and encouragement from Derek—and even there, he'd improved a lot over the years they'd known each other.

What did surprise Derek was that Vijay had only one book in his hands as they lined up to check out their finds. Derek was loaded down with seven books on addiction—everything from a memoir by a well-known basketball player about his days as a drug addict, to psychology books by people like Dr. Sigmund Freud.

"That's all you're taking out?" Derek asked his friend.

"Oh, this? This isn't a library book. It's a cheat book for *Super Mario Brothers*. I bought it with my allowance last week."

"Oh." Derek was totally taken aback.

"I'll come back for research books when I start on the paper," Vijay said. "Maybe next week or the week after. It shouldn't take too long to write it. Only six pages, after all."

"*Only* six pages?" Derek repeated, shaking his head. Vijay sure seemed confident that he'd have plenty of time to accomplish the task. Then again, he wasn't going to be playing ball practically every day after school, like Derek.

"Should be a breeze," Vijay concluded. "Need help carrying those?"

"Nah, I've got it," said Derek as they went outside to hop the late bus back to Mount Royal Townhouses.

"Hey, now that you've got all your materials together, how about taking a break from work this afternoon?" Vijay said.

Derek looked out the bus window. "It's going to start raining any second."

"So never mind playing ball on the Hill. How about coming over to my house later? We can play some *Mario Brothers* and stuff."

It did sound like fun. Derek had only played video games

a couple of times on other kids' consoles, and not for very long. Besides, he had been working hard—two separate practices that week, one for each team. "Okay, I'll ask my dad if I can come over after I finish my homework," he told Vijay.

Mr. Jeter was happy to let Derek go over to Vijay's until dinnertime, as long as Vijay and Derek spent some time discussing their term papers.

Which they *did* intend to do. At least, Derek did. Vijay's advice on school projects always came in handy.

"So, about our term papers," Derek said while Vijay booted up the game system.

"What about them?"

"Isn't everybody going to be basically writing the same thing? 'Drugs are bad,' et cetera?"

"Probably," Vijay said. "So what?"

"You know Mr. L will probably make us get up there and read them out loud," Derek reminded him. "He almost always does. Man, I hate that part."

"So, write about something else," Vijay suggested.

"Huh?"

"Other kinds of addictions. You know, like gambling, drinking, smoking . . ."

"Hmmm." Derek liked that idea, even though it meant he might have to go back to the library and take out even more books.

"Now, that's enough about school and work," Vijay said. "Here. You're Mario. I'm Luigi. Let's play."

Derek would have liked to talk more about the school project, and maybe nail down a specific addiction that only he would be writing about.

But the little Mario character kept hopping up and down, making noises as if to say, *Come on now. Start me running.*

Derek sighed, and he gave up thinking about the addictions paper. His attention went instead to the little mustachioed man on the screen. And for the next while, he and Vijay lost themselves in game play, conquering level after level, beating boss after boss . . . until . . .

"Whoa. What time is it?" Derek suddenly realized that a lot of time must have gone by.

"Five to six," Vijay replied, checking the wristwatch he always wore.

"Noooo! I'm going to be late," Derek said, laying down the controller and springing to his feet. "I can't believe it. Were we really playing for *two hours*?"

"We were indeed," Vijay said, grinning. "See you tomorrow, then?"

"Nah, I've got baseball. Soon, though." And Derek was out the door in a flash, running full speed through the raindrops, until he was back home.

The whole family looked up at him from their seats at the dinner table. "Well," said Mrs. Jeter. "Look who decided to show up for supper." She looked at the clock. It said 6:05. Yes, he was late by only five minutes. But still, he was late, and in the Jeter house at dinnertime, that was a violation.

"Sorry, Mom. Sorry, Dad. I just lost track of time. It won't happen again, I promise."

His dad frowned. "It'd better not, Derek," he said.

"Sorry," Derek repeated. "We just got busy with stuff, and it was really involving . . ." He didn't mention that what they'd been involved in was video games, not studying.

He sat down, and they all started eating. Derek didn't say a word. He just hoped the talk would turn to something else besides his being late for dinner.

His mom finally said, "Jeter, I brought home some spec sheets from the Realtor's office."

"Oh good," said Mr. Jeter. "We can go over them later."

"What's a spec sheet?" Sharlee asked. "A sheet with specks all over it?"

Mrs. Jeter laughed. "No, Sharlee," she said. "A spec sheet is a sheet with specific information. In this case it's about houses."

"So what are the specks?" Sharlee said, still not getting it.

"Well, how much the house rents for, for instance. And how big it is, and where it's located, and how many bedrooms there are—"

"Okay, okay," Derek said, feeling suddenly irritated. "We get it."

"Calm down, Derek," said his father. "Your mother's talking to your sister, not to you."

"Are there pictures of the houses?" Sharlee wanted to know.

"There sure are," said Mrs. Jeter.

"Can I see them?" Sharlee begged. "Please? Pleeeze?"

"Sure, why not? But first let's finish our dinner."

Soon after they cleared the table, everyone but Derek was looking over the spec sheets for half a dozen houses. "Ooo, look!" Sharlee kept saying, pointing out one feature or another. "I want this bedroom to be mine, okay? I love that picture window. Look. There's a big tree in the back-yard. Daddy, you could build me a tree house!"

Derek rolled his eyes. Sharlee was lost in her fantasies. For him, though, moving away was a terrifying reality, a hur-ricane about to slam into his life and blow it to smithereens.

He noticed, for instance, that all the addresses of the houses were in neighborhoods that were too far to walk to from Mount Royal Townhouses. *Why do they have to look at places so far away?* he wondered. *Aren't there any nice houses in this part of town?*

He wanted to raise his voice and object to the whole idea of moving. But he kept silent. He'd already annoyed his parents by being late. Now was not the time to annoy them any further.

Still, he knew he'd have to say something eventually—and sooner rather than later—if he wanted to convince them to stay put. Something like: "Mount Royal is my home, and it always will be. Don't rip me away from it!"

Chapter Four

BIG LEAGUE, LITTLE LEAGUE

His Little League team, the Reds, was a nice bunch of kids. Derek already knew a few of them: Elliott Koppel, Norman Nelson, Ernesto Alvarez.

They all had one thing in common, though. None of them was very athletic. They'd improved since Derek had first played with them, but not that much, as far as he could tell.

That didn't matter so much to Derek. In fact, at their first practice the previous Wednesday, he'd had more fun than at travel team practice. Because there was no pressure on him, he'd just relaxed and enjoyed himself.

Most of the kids on the Reds were there to have fun and get some exercise. There were a few who were laser-focused on winning, like Derek, but not everyone was on that wavelength. Derek had noticed right away that here, unlike on the travel team, kids weren't backing one another up, or covering bases, or throwing to the cutoff man.

He missed Vijay. They'd shared so many good times on the ball field. And none of his other friends were on this team.

Today, Saturday, was the Reds' first game. Watching their opponents' batting practice, Derek thought the Dodgers looked beatable.

The Reds' coach, a really nice guy named Herb Hamilton, was the father of the team's pitcher, Zeke, whom Derek remembered hitting against in previous seasons.

Standing at shortstop, Derek watched Zeke warm up. The guy threw hard, but he had trouble controlling the ball. He walked the first two Dodger hitters, notching only one strike along the way.

The Reds shouted encouragement, doing their part to steady Zeke's nerves. Charlie Morgenstern, over at third base, yelled the loudest. Zeke must have heard him, because he threw the next pitch right over the heart of the plate.

The hitter swatted a hard ground ball right at Charlie, who grabbed it, then tried to tag the runner going from second to third—but missed. He then threw to first, but it was too late. Everyone was safe.

Bases loaded, nobody out. Zeke and the Reds were digging themselves into a gigantic hole. Derek bounced lightly on the balls of his feet, pounding his glove, willing the ball to come his way.

CRACK!

Derek's reflexes kicked into gear as the sizzling line drive threatened to hit him right in the face. He raised his mitt and snagged the ball at the last instant, just before it hit the ground. Then, seeing that the runner on third had started for home, he fired it to Charlie, who stepped on third before the runner could get back to the bag to complete the double play.

"Woo-hoo!" Coach Herb yelled, clapping his hands. "What a play."

"Way to go, Derek!"

"Great play!"

"Attaboy."

All his teammates shouted at once.

Derek held up two fingers, reminding his teammates of how many outs there were—and to remind them that they needed to get one more out to finish off this half inning.

Zeke walked the next batter to reload the bases. Then he hit the next one, forcing in the Dodgers' first run.

"Come on, Zeke," Derek shouted. "You've got this!" He just wanted Zeke to get the ball over, trusting his teammates to make a play.

Zeke did get the ball over. But the hitter slammed it into

right field, where it got past Elliott. Two more runs scored, and it was now 3–0, with runners at second and third.

At least the next batter struck out to end the inning. A 3–0 hole was not impossible to climb out of, Derek told himself—not this early in the game.

Coach Herb's lineup had Derek hitting cleanup, probably because at practice Derek had launched moon rockets all over the field.

George Eng led off for the Reds with a bunt single. George was still waiting for his growth spurt to start. But he sure could run the bases. Two pitches later George was standing on third base.

Leadoff man? Sure, Derek thought. *Why not?*

Luckily for the Reds, the Dodgers' pitcher was no more accurate than Zeke. By the time Derek came to the plate, the pitcher had walked Charlie and Zeke to load the bases.

Part of Derek wanted to hit a long ball and start the season with a grand slam. But he also knew that the pitcher was having trouble getting it over, and therefore, it was best to wait for his pitch before swinging.

He watched two fastballs and two changeups go by. Now the count was 2–2, and it was anybody's guess what was coming next.

Derek focused intently on the pitcher's hand. He saw the release of the ball and identified it as a changeup. After holding back his swing for a full second, he let it rip.

BOOM!

"Go, go, go!" Coach Herb yelled as Derek rounded first base. By the time the right fielder threw the ball back in, Derek was already standing at second, being applauded by everyone, including the two runners he'd just driven in.

Ernesto was up next. He grounded out, but that brought Zeke in with the Reds' third run and sent Derek to third.

Now it was Elliott's turn. He hit a hard line drive, but the pitcher stuck out his glove and snagged it for the second out. Then Norman struck out to end the frame.

"All right! We tied it up," Coach Herb said excitedly. "Now let's hold 'em. C'mon, Zeke, buckle down. You've got this."

Zeke dug at the front of the rubber with his heel, making it easier to push off the mound. It seemed to make his ball a little faster, and more accurate, too. Zeke struck out the number nine hitter before facing the leadoff batter for the second time.

The hitter had seen Zeke once, but the ball was coming out of his hand faster now. The batter took two strikes, both on fastballs over the heart of the plate.

"Attaway, Zeke," Derek shouted, pounding his mitt.

Zeke reared back and threw what looked like his fastest pitch yet—but it wasn't. It was a wicked changeup, and the hitter swung right through it. And he followed that up with another strikeout for good measure!

"A one, two, three inning," Derek said, clapping Zeke

on the back as they returned to the dugout.

The score stayed tied as the Reds put two men on in their half of the second, but went down without scoring. Derek watched the last out from the on-deck circle. He'd have to wait one more inning for his next at bat.

In the third inning Zeke lost the plate again, walking the first two hitters before striking out the next. Then he gave up a monster shot, a long fly ball to center that Derek felt sure would be caught—but George dropped the ball, and everybody came around to score. 6–3, Dodgers.

Zeke rallied to retire the next two hitters, one on a bloop fly that Derek caught over his shoulder in shallow left field.

"Hey," Coach Herb yelled, clapping. "There's our MVP."

Derek pretended he hadn't heard him. But the words were still ringing in his ears as he led off with a sharp line drive that got by the right fielder and kept on rolling. Derek flew around the bases. And when the relay throw got past the third baseman, he continued on home, scoring the team's fourth run on an inside-the-parker!

After getting mobbed by his excited teammates, Derek took a seat on the bench to catch his breath, while he watched the rest of the team's turn at bat.

He wished the coach hadn't said what he'd said. What would the other kids think, hearing him say Derek was the MVP?

Through all his years in Little League, Derek had

always been one of the better players, sometimes one of the top three, but there'd always been others who'd gotten named MVP, except once.

And here the coach was already anointing him—in their first game. Derek hoped it wouldn't jinx him. But it sure put more pressure on him to perform. Especially since, as he was going to tell the coach after the game, Derek had scheduling conflicts and would have to miss about half their games. Would Coach Herb still call him the MVP then?

Derek's attention was called back to the game when his teammates hopped off the bench, cheering. Norman had just hit a double. Derek looked at the scoreboard and saw that there were two outs. He'd been so lost in his own thoughts that he'd actually missed Ernesto's and Elliott's at bats.

"Let's go," he shouted, then cheered again as Norman stole third on a passed ball. But the rally died right there, as the next hitter, first baseman Ben Tabor, struck out swinging.

In the fourth inning Charlie and Zeke switched positions.

"Nice job," Derek called over to third base.

"Thanks," Zeke said, nodding. "You too."

Charlie struck out the side. Unfortunately, those three strikeouts came with four walks mixed in. Now it was 7–4, Dodgers.

In the bottom of the fourth, Derek came to bat for the third time with two out and men on first and third. He jumped on the first pitch—a fastball up in his eyes—and lashed a double down the left field line, driving in both runners, and narrowing the deficit to 7–6.

He then stole third on a wild pitch, and scored when Ernesto beat out a slow grounder down the third baseline. Tie ball game, 7–7!

Elliott then flied out to end the inning, but now the game was totally up for grabs.

Derek stopped at the mound on his way out to short. "Come on, Charlie," he said. "Let's do this."

Charlie nodded, pulled down the visor of his cap, and turned to the plate, concentrating. He blew away the first hitter with fastballs. Then he started changing speeds, fooling the next hitter into popping up. He finished off the inning with a foul pop-up that Ernesto, the catcher, caught before it hit the ground.

Derek didn't get to hit in the fifth. The Reds went down easily, with just one walk.

Luckily, Charlie held the lead in the sixth, walking two men but also getting two fly balls and a clutch strikeout.

Now, in the bottom of the sixth, the game was there to be won. It was all laid out before the Reds on a silver platter—and Derek was due up third.

The Reds all cheered for Charlie and Zeke, but it didn't do any good. They both grounded out weakly to the pitcher.

Derek desperately wanted to end this game right now, so they wouldn't have to go into extra innings. As much as he wanted to end it with one swing, however, he knew that if he tried to hit a home run, he was less likely to than if he just tried to hit the ball hard somewhere.

The first pitch was a looping curveball. Derek didn't try to do too much with it. He just reached out and flicked it over the shortstop's head for a single. It was a hit he was pretty sure he could have caught if he'd been out there. But he was happy to get on base.

When the next pitch got away from the catcher, Derek stole a base. Now he was in scoring position.

Ernesto pounded his bat head on the plate and took a few fierce practice swings.

"Just a base hit," Derek shouted. "That's all we need."

Had Ernesto heard him? Or was he going to strike out trying to kill the ball?

With the count at 2–0, Ernesto swung for the fences. He barely hit the ball off the end of the bat, producing a blooper over the first baseman's head.

Derek was running on contact, with two outs. He was already rounding third when the ball landed fair, and he easily crossed the plate with the winning run!

The Reds' bench exploded in happy chaos as they all high-fived one another to celebrate their victory.

And Derek was right in the middle of it. He was happy in the moment. He'd powered his team to a victory they might not have gotten without him. He'd had fun, too, as he always did playing ball.

But it still wasn't the same without Vijay there.

"So, what did you want to talk to me about?" Coach Herb said after the hubbub had died down.

"Huh?"

"You know, before the game? You said you wanted to tell me something?"

"Oh yeah." Derek sheepishly pulled his travel team schedule out of his back pocket. "It turns out I have a ton of conflicts. I'm going to have to miss a lot of games, Coach."

Coach took the schedule and looked at it. "Wow," he said, sounding deflated. "Looks like you're going to miss . . . wow . . . half our games?"

"Something like that," Derek said. "I'm really sorry, Coach. I feel like I'm letting down the team."

"Well," Coach Herb said with a sigh, "it's going to be tough without our MVP." He paused as Derek winced. "But we'll just do the best we can and try to fight through it." He shrugged. "You did tell me you had travel team, and that it was a priority for you."

Derek just hung his head, feeling guilty.

"I just never thought it would mean missing this many games. . . ."

Other kids had gathered, and the whispers were going

around, explaining what Derek had said. The players all looked like they'd been hit by a truck. Gone was the celebration of five minutes before, replaced by an atmosphere of gloom.

Derek sat there, feeling like a bad teammate. Sure, he'd just helped them win this game, so nobody was going to say anything. But what were they feeling, deep down inside? Were they mad at him? Disappointed?

He knew he would have felt that way. He knew how he *did* feel, and it wasn't good.

He wished it hadn't turned out like this, but what could he do about it?

Chapter Five
FANTASY AND REALITY

"I don't know why you always have to miss my games," Sharlee complained to Derek as they sat at the table eating ham-and-cheese sandwiches. "You could have come."

"No, I couldn't," Derek corrected her. "My game wasn't over until twelve thirty, and then I had to see the coach about my schedule."

"You still could have gotten there by the third inning or so," she said, pressing the issue. "It was great. We won by, like, a million runs. And I hit a homer, just like I told you I would."

"That's great, Sharlee," Derek said, genuinely proud of her. "Sorry I was busy."

"You're *always* busy," she shot back.

"Hey, I hit a home run too, by the way."

"Don't brag," she said, crossing her arms. "It's not nice."

Derek had to laugh. "Okay, okay. And you didn't see *my* game, either, so I say we're even."

"But everyone else's big brother was there!"

"Sorry. I'll get to at least one or two of your games this season, I promise." He sure hoped he would be able to, but the truth was, he had no idea when he'd have the time.

"You all about ready?" Mr. Jeter asked.

"Wait, what?" Derek said. "Ready for what?"

"We're going house-hunting this afternoon, old man," his mom reminded him. "We told you, remember?"

"No," said Derek, semi-truthfully. He vaguely recalled the subject coming up, but he hadn't been paying attention. "Do I have to go?" The last thing he wanted to do with his free Sunday afternoon was look at houses with a real estate agent.

"Moving to a house is not a disaster, Derek," said his father sternly. "You might like having more space, your own backyard, things like that."

No. He *wouldn't.* He loved it *here.* What was so wrong with Mount Royal that his parents wanted to move, anyway? So what if it was small? It was what he was *used* to.

Then he had an idea. "Can I go over to Vijay's instead? I've barely had any time to see him lately."

"Hmmm," his mother said, frowning. "Jeter?"

"He really should come with us, Dot. This is a major family decision."

"You can pick out a few houses you like, and I'll come see them later," Derek suggested.

His parents looked at each other meaningfully. "Did Vijay invite you?"

"He's always home Sundays 'cause his parents have off work. I can call and see if it's okay."

"All right," said his mother. "On one condition."

"What?"

"You've both got that big paper for school, right? How about you put in some time on it while you're together?"

"Do I have to?"

"If you want to be excused from going with the rest of us, you do," said Mr. Jeter. "That's a big project you've got there, and you've already got a heavy baseball schedule cutting into your time. You know what they say about procrastination, right?"

"Procasta what?" Sharlee asked.

"It means 'putting off till tomorrow what you should be doing today,'" Derek explained.

"Exactly," said Mr. Jeter.

"And that's *bad*?" Sharlee asked, confused.

"All right, Dad," Derek said. "I promise. Can I call Vijay now?"

"All right," said his mom.

He dialed, and as Derek had expected, Vijay was more

than happy to have him come over, even when Derek told him about having to do schoolwork.

"Have a great time," he told his folks as he gathered his library books and notebook and stuffed them into his book bag. "See you at dinner. Thanks, Mom. Thanks, Dad."

As he ran out the door, he heard an annoyed Sharlee complain, "How come he doesn't want to come with us?"

"All right, that's enough work for one day," Vijay said, putting down his library book and stretching his arms and legs.

Derek looked at the clock on the wall. "Really? We've only been doing this for twenty minutes."

"Who's counting?"

Derek thought about it. Technically they *had* done work, although Derek himself had just been getting into the material he'd checked out of the school library. It was titled *Sugar: The Deadly Poison*.

"Are you any closer to choosing a subject?" Vijay asked.

Derek shook his head. "There are so many," he reflected. "Things are called addictions that I never even thought of. I even took out a book called *Addicted to Sugar: A Life in Baking*. Did you know sugar could be an addiction?"

"Wow," said Vijay. "Hey, if you don't do that one, can I?"

"Sure," said Derek.

"Gary Parnell told me he's doing his on sports addiction," Vijay said.

"Surprise, surprise," said Derek sarcastically. Sports

and Gary went together like fire and water.

"So, what do you say we play some video games?" Vijay suggested.

"Okay," said Derek, still feeling that they ought to be spending more time on their papers. His parents would definitely not be pleased if they knew how little time he'd put in.

But the temptation was too great, at least for Vijay. And Derek was a guest, after all. He figured he should go along with the host's plan.

Besides, playing *Super Mario Brothers* sure was fun. And there were dozens of other video games, according to Vijay, all here in his living room.

Before Derek knew it, they'd been playing for two and a half hours. Derek was in the middle of a particularly challenging level, climbing magic beanstalks, busting brick blocks, and collecting coins and mushrooms, when the phone rang.

"Keep playing," Vijay told him. "I'll get it."

Vijay went to answer it. "Hello? Oh, hi, Mrs. Jeter. How are you and Mr. Jeter? How is Sharlee?" Vijay motioned to Derek, holding his hand over the phone. "Keep playing. I'll stall them. You have to finish the level."

Vijay then went on to have a conversation with Derek's mom, telling her all about the Patel family's week in India, while Derek frantically maneuvered the controller, and finally bopped the big boss and jumped onto the flagpole to complete the level. Then he put down the controller and took the phone from Vijay.

"Hi, Mom," he said. "What's up?"

"We're on our way back, and we've picked up pizza, so wrap it up over there and be home in fifteen minutes, okay?"

"Sure, Mom."

"Did you guys get any work done?"

"Some," Derek said casually.

"Great. What is that music I'm hearing in the background? Are you boys watching TV?"

"Sort of. We were taking a break from work." It was true—*kind of*—although, that didn't stop Derek from feeling like he'd done something he shouldn't have.

"I've got to go," he told Vijay after hanging up. "They're bringing pizza and it'll get cold."

"Okay, I'll save your game for you."

"See you tomorrow at the bus stop," Derek said.

"See you." Vijay was already engrossed in playing the game. He didn't even turn around as Derek left for home.

Derek hoisted his book bag and carried the heavy load across the whole length of Mount Royal Townhouses. Thinking about what had just happened gave him a great idea, one that wouldn't need any of the library books he'd checked out. The subject was one he could research personally—addiction to *video games*.

The pizza smelled delicious, and Derek dug in along with the rest of them.

"We saw so many houses," Sharlee said excitedly. "One of them had a bathroom that was totally pink."

"Great," Derek said unenthusiastically.

"We did see three houses that were pretty wonderful," Mrs. Jeter said, exchanging a twinkling glance with her husband. "They had a handout with pictures we can show you after dinner, Derek."

Derek sighed. He'd been hoping, somehow, that actually *seeing* other places would make his parents realize how great Mount Royal was and what a big mistake it would be to move.

But obviously that wasn't going to happen. They were more excited than ever about moving away. Derek's mood totally tanked.

He didn't *want* to move. Why didn't that seem to matter to his parents? Didn't they care what he thought? Besides, all those so-called wonderful houses were probably crummy anyway.

Chapter Six
LOSING THE GROOVE

After two practices with his travel team, the West Siders, Derek had already improved a ton—everything from pickoff plays at second, to rundowns, bunting, hit-and-run plays, hitting the cutoff man, positioning yourself for relay throws . . .

Everyone on the team was a quick learner. And now they were finally getting the chance to put all that knowledge to work in an actual game.

Their opponents were the Lakers, from Comstock, a nearby town. They'd come to Kalamazoo by car caravan, something Derek and his teammates would be doing for their next game. He was glad that, at least for today, the West Siders were the home team.

The visitors' stands were half full of parents who had made the trip. On the first-base side the stands were crammed with West Siders fans—amazing for a Wednesday late afternoon. Derek's whole family was there, sitting on the highest tier of the stands. Sharlee was there with her friends the Parker triplets, who were here because their brothers, Christian and Daxon, were on the team with Derek.

Sharlee waved to him, and he waved back, just as the umpire yelled, "Play ball!" Derek settled into his ready position as the leadoff hitter stepped into the batter's box.

This had a different feel from a Little League game. Derek wasn't sure what it was, but it felt like he'd been promoted from AAA to the major leagues. The tension was much higher, and the game hadn't even started.

Derek blew out a big breath and shook out his arms and legs to get rid of some of the nervousness he was feeling. Then he crouched down a bit, pounding his glove and bouncing up and down on the balls of his feet.

Derek looked around from his position at short.

To his right was Brad Russell at third base. The coach's son, he'd been on the travel team ever since he was old enough to qualify. To Derek's left was Mohammed "Mo" Salem at second, another travel team veteran. The team was studded with them—Nate Wallace at first; Daxon Parker in left; his brother, Christian, in right. . . . They all had more travel team experience than Derek or Harry.

There were three other new kids. Two of them had joined the team last fall along with Derek and Harry—Landon August behind the plate, and Eli Warren, the team's alternate. The third newbie had only come on board this spring. Mason Adams, Derek's old teammate, was in the same center field spot he'd always manned in Little League.

"Let's go," Derek called to Harry, clapping his mitt. Harry toed the rubber, focused intently on the plate, and let the first pitch fly.

"Strike one!"

Derek relaxed just a bit. Now that the game was on, he found he could focus better, and not be as distracted by the butterflies in his stomach that he'd had leading up to the game. He was actually starting to enjoy the extra pressure. He felt more alert and on his toes now.

"Strike two!"

"Go, Harry," Derek shouted. "Yeah!"

The hitter, who had let the first two fastballs go by, swung at the third pitch and hit it to left-center for a single. Derek took the relay throw and tossed it back to Harry.

"Don't worry, you've got this," Derek told him. Harry nodded in agreement and went back to work.

The Lakers looked good in their bright blue uniforms. They looked like athletes. And they hit like athletes too. The next batter shot the ball into right, and it dropped in front of Christian, who threw to third to hold the runner at second.

Still nobody out. Derek and the rest of the West Siders kept on calling out encouraging words. But Harry was looking increasingly worried. Before he could face the next hitter, Coach Russell bounded off the bench and went to talk to him. Derek took a few steps closer so he could hear what was said.

"You've got to slow things down," the coach told Harry. "Take deep breaths, get your heart to stop pounding. It's making you overthrow it, and your fastball is straightening out. Relax, take a little bit off the fastball, and you'll get the movement back on it."

Harry nodded, and the coach went back to the bench. His words seemed to turn the tide. Harry struck out the next two batters, although the runners did move up on a passed ball by Landon and ended up on second and third with two out.

Up came the number-five hitter, a gigantic kid with a powerful frame. His practice swings were vicious, and Derek could see beads of sweat trickling down Harry's neck.

Harry started off with a changeup that the batter swung right through for strike one. Another changeup, another strike on a foul back to the screen.

"Whew," Derek muttered under his breath. "He just missed that one."

Harry must have realized that too, because the next pitch was a fastball. But the hitter was ready for it. He hit it right on the barrel, and right at Derek.

Derek's reflexes took over. He ducked, looked away from the oncoming missile, stuck out his glove . . . and snagged it for the out, saving two runs.

"Yeah!" yelled Harry, and the team ran back to the bench, excited and relieved—none more so than Derek.

He'd been tested right at the outset, and he'd survived his baptism by fire. It was a good start to the season, and it felt fantastic. He couldn't wait to get up to the plate and show off the hitting prowess he'd developed over the winter. After his 4 for 4 in the Little League game last Saturday, he felt like he was in a real groove at the plate.

Mason led off for the West Siders. He was late on two fastballs, but then a changeup hit him in the arm and he took first base, rubbing the sore spot and wincing. Derek shook his head. *Imagine if it had been a fastball,* he thought. Mason could have really gotten hurt.

Nate was up next. The pitcher fired fastball after fastball, and Nate kept fouling them off. Finally, though, he whiffed on a changeup, fooled by the speed.

Derek came up to the plate, feeling good about his chances. Fastballs were his favorite pitch to hit. And this was a fastball pitcher, for sure. In fact, he was throwing harder than anyone else Derek had ever faced.

Derek let the first one go by to gauge the speed, and knew he would have to hurry his swing to catch up to it. The second pitch buzzed his head, and he had to duck to avoid getting crowned by the ball!

The third pitch was a changeup, and Derek was way out in front. The swing he took made him look silly, and the Lakers bench erupted in cheers and hoots. Those cheers got even louder when Derek swung through a fastball for strike three.

He walked back to the bench, stunned and deflated. He'd been so sure he'd had that last pitch timed, yet he'd missed it.

He sat back down on the bench, feeling miserable. He barely watched as Harry grounded out to first to end the frame.

Derek was still thinking about his at bat during the next inning at shortstop. Instead of his head being in the moment, he was running over that last pitch again and again in his mind.

At just that instant the batter hit a sharp grounder to Derek's right. Derek was late reacting because it took him a fraction of a second to switch his focus. And in that instant an out turned into a hit—or more accurately, an error.

His first error of the season, in only the second inning of their first game. Derek felt a wave of embarrassment wash over him. He knew he should have been paying better attention. He'd let his mind wander, and now it might cost his team.

He promised himself he wouldn't let it happen again, no matter what.

Unfortunately, the next batter walked, and after Harry

notched a pair of strikeouts, a ringing double to left scored two runs. Derek winced. One of those had been his fault. He promised himself he would get that run back for his team the next time he came to bat.

Harry struck out the next hitter, but now the West Siders were down 2–0. They needed to get their offense working, fast.

Mo led off the inning with an infield hit that he beat out with sheer speed. That was the thing about Mo, Derek thought. He was tall, and he had filled out over the winter, so he wasn't as skinny as he'd been last fall. But he hadn't lost any of his speed. In fact, by the time Brad struck out, Mo had already stolen second and third.

Next up was Daxon. He was big and strong, with long hair that stuck out under the batting helmet. He didn't always connect with the ball, but when he did, it went a long way. This time he got a hold of one and hit it to left, over the shortstop's head. Mo was motoring, and Derek yelled excitedly as Mo slid into home, just ahead of the relay throw, for the team's first run!

Daxon should have been on second base, but he'd slipped rounding first and had had to hold up there. Had he been on second, he would have scored when the next hitter, Christian, laced a sharp grounder past the first baseman for a clean double. Instead the West Siders had men on second and third, with only one out.

Landon walked to load the bases. But they ran out of

luck when Mason sent a line drive right into the pitcher's mitt. Daxon was caught off third base, and the pitcher fired over there to complete the double play. Derek moaned in frustration, along with the rest of his teammates. They'd been so close to taking the lead!

"Derek," Coach Russell said as Derek grabbed his glove to go back out there. "You're in left this inning."

"*What?* But, Coach—"

But the coach had already moved on. "Daxon, you're on third. Brad, over to short."

Derek sighed and trotted slowly out to left field, doing as he'd been told but not happy about it at all. Coach Russell had said he was going to shuffle players around to different positions. But Derek had never imagined he'd be switched away from shortstop so fast. Derek had to believe it was because he'd made that error last inning. He could have kicked himself over it.

It felt weird being in the outfield. If a ball was hit to him, would he get a good read on it, quickly enough to track it down? He could feel his self-confidence waver and wobble, and it sure didn't feel good.

Baseball being baseball, the first batter sent a fly ball over Derek's head. He chased it down, but not before the hitter was on second base with a leadoff double. That led to two more runs, and now the West Siders were down by a score of 4–1. The half inning ended without further scoring, but the damage had been done.

Nate led off the West Siders' half of the third with a walk. Derek came to the plate determined to drive him in. He wanted to make up for the run he'd cost his team with that error. He wanted it so badly that he swung way too hard, missing a ball that was up at his eye level.

"Calm down," he ordered himself. "Forget the error. Focus on the pitch."

The fans in the stands were yelling, and so were his teammates. The team needed a hit, and everyone expected him to deliver—himself most of all.

The next pitch was a changeup, and Derek was way out in front. "Too anxious," he scolded himself under his breath. "Come on now."

The third pitch was a fastball right down the middle. Derek gave it everything he had, and fouled it off. The next pitch looked low to him, and he held up.

"Strike three!" the umpire said.

"What?" Derek could not believe it, but he knew never to argue with an umpire. His dad had always taught him to show respect to everyone, especially adults—*especially* adults in positions of authority, like umps.

Derek trudged sadly back to the bench, while everyone else directed their cheers toward Harry, the next West Siders batter. He came through, hitting a long home run to center that made the score 4–3.

Derek forgot all about his own troubles, leaping to his feet. "Yeah, Harry! We're right back in this thing." There was still time to come back and win this game—plenty of time. When Mo and Daxon walked, it looked like the West Siders were about to take the lead.

But Brad popped out to short, and Christian struck out to end the third. And the score remained stuck at 4–3 through the next two innings.

Harry stayed strong through the fourth. In the bottom of the inning the West Siders put two men on with one out, and Derek got another RBI opportunity. He made contact this time but only managed a pop fly to first. Harry walked to load the bases for the West Siders. But the team came up short again when Mo hit a grounder to second for the final out.

Derek was relieved when Coach Russell put him back at short for the fifth. Mo came in to relieve Harry, and Harry went over to second base. Mo held the Lakers scoreless, giving up only a harmless two-out single.

In their half of the inning, the West Siders amazingly loaded the bases again, with two outs—and *again* failed to score. Derek could only watch in frustration from the on-deck circle as Nate struck out to end the inning.

Mo was having himself a day on the mound, luckily. He struck out the side in the sixth, and so the West Siders still had a decent shot as they took their last licks, with Derek leading off for his fourth at bat of the day.

Whatever happened, Derek swore to himself he would not strike out for a third time. He'd never struck out three times in a single game in his entire life, and he didn't mean to start now.

The ump called the first pitch a strike—even though it was outside. It was all Derek could do not to complain about it. But he collected himself and got ready for the next pitch.

It was inside, and low. Derek leapt to try to get out of the way, but it hit him right in the calf. "OWW!" he yelled, grabbing it and hobbling around.

Coach Russell came out of the dugout toward him, but Derek waved him off. His calf hurt, all right, but not that badly.

Harry took the first pitch for a strike. The second pitch was low, and the ball got away from the catcher. Derek, who moments ago had been wincing in pain, suddenly took off like a shot for second base.

"He's going," the Laker second baseman yelled to the catcher. The catcher, startled, threw the ball way over the second baseman's head—and Derek was off and running again. He wound up on third base, laughing as the West Siders and their fans erupted in cheers.

When Harry hit the next pitch for a single, Derek waltzed home with the tying run, and was mobbed by his teammates. Now he got to watch and cheer as Mo bunted Harry to second. Brad flied out to center, but Daxon, with two out, got the winning hit—a clean single to right, and the West Siders poured onto the field to celebrate their opening-day win, 5–4!

Everyone else was ecstatic, but Derek had distinctly mixed feelings. He was happy for his team but not at all happy about his own performance. He hadn't had his usual success at the plate, and he'd let it get to him, to the point where it had affected his play in the field. The only good thing he'd done was to steal that base.

Well, at least he'd contributed something to the victory, he told himself. At the next game he'd do better. All he had to do was wait till Saturday morning, and he could show everyone what his A game was all about.

Funny about his hitting, though. It had been going so well all winter, and at the Little League game. Strange how his skills had deserted him like that, especially when he'd been feeling so good at the plate. . . .

Chapter Seven

HOOKED?

Derek stood beside the bus on Friday after classes, scanning the school exit doors as other kids passed him and climbed in.

Where was Vijay? Usually his friend was the one waiting for *him*.

A group of kids was coming slowly toward him from the cafeteria exit. Wait—was that *Vijay* with them?

It *was*. Vijay was in animated conversation with four other boys, and none of them was watching where they were going. Nor did they seem in a hurry to get onto their buses and head home. Other kids jostled to hurry past them, but they didn't seem to notice.

"Hey, Vij," Derek called out. Vijay saw him, waved, and

went right back to his conversation with the other boys.

Derek didn't want the bus to leave without him, so he got on and sat near the back, saving the seat next to him for Vijay—if he ever made it.

The driver beeped her horn, startling everyone. She, too, seemed to be losing patience. Finally Vijay got on and made his way down the aisle. Sitting down next to Derek, he waved out the window to the three other boys.

One of them, Derek noticed, was Harry Hicks. To Derek's surprise, another was Gary Parnell, the class brainiac.

Derek and Gary had a long history, as rivals vying for the best grades, opponents in debates about sports (which Gary hated), even reluctant teammates in Little League. Vijay had never had much use for Gary in the past. *Are the two of them friends now?* Derek wondered.

Vijay had a big smile on his face. "Derek!" he said breathlessly. "Do you want to go to the arcade tomorrow afternoon? Everybody's going."

"Who's everyone? *Those* guys?" Derek nodded toward Gary and the others.

"Yes. And a couple more kids from Mount Royal too," Vijay said. "But don't worry, there are plenty of game consoles there. The place is very gigantic. You will love it for sure!"

Now Derek understood why Vijay and the others were so excited. He thought of all the money he'd saved up over Christmas, and from doing chores all spring. He'd saved more than enough to spend a small portion of it at the arcade. . . .

"For sure," he told Vijay. "I mean, unless travel team goes into extra innings or something. I should be done by then."

"Same for Harry," Vijay pointed out. "Maybe you guys could get driven over there together."

"Yeah. Maybe." *If* his parents said *yes*, that was. But Derek was pretty sure they'd let him, so long as he promised to get his schoolwork done tonight.

Maybe Vijay had been right not to take out too many books, Derek thought, staring at the pile of addiction books in front of him.

He started reading, and he was shocked to discover that there was apparently a whole group of young people who never left their rooms at all, because they were so addicted to playing video games.

Derek really wanted to join Vijay and his other friends tomorrow at the arcade. He was excited to check out all the cool new games. But if he did, would he risk becoming one of those kids who never came out of their rooms, even to eat?

"That's ridiculous," he told himself. "I don't believe it. And even if it's true, it would never happen to *me*."

Besides, he really, *really* wanted to go tomorrow—not because he was addicted but just because it was *so much fun*.

There was a soft knock on his bedroom door, and Derek

looked up to see his father standing there, smiling. "Nice to see you cracking the books," Mr. Jeter said approvingly. "How's it going?"

"Oh, fine," Derek said wearily.

"You don't *sound* like it's fine. What's going on, Derek? You look miserable."

"Oh, Dad," Derek said, sighing, "I just can't decide what to write about. There are too many choices, and I don't really know much about any of them."

His dad picked up a couple of the books and read their titles. "Addictions, huh? Well, that's something I know a little about."

Mr. Jeter was now a certified alcohol and drug counselor, and Derek was sure he knew much more than a little about it.

"Do you think you could help me write my paper?" he asked.

"Now, I *know* you don't mean that," said his dad.

"Well, not *write* it, but at least give me some pointers?"

"It's good that you're not too personally familiar with addictions at your age," said Mr. Jeter. "Or at any age, for that matter. But you've got to know enough to steer clear of them, and they're not always the obvious ones everybody knows about."

He held up a book titled *Addicted to Sugar: A Life in Baking.*

"Are you saying I'm addicted to sugar?" Derek asked.

"Mmmm," said his dad, grinning. "Well, I know you like your desserts, but that doesn't make you a sugar addict."

"So how do I choose what to write about?"

"Well, you may not be addicted to anything, but surely you feel tempted. We all do. Maybe some of your friends are finding certain things hard to resist."

Suddenly it came to Derek—how to ask for what he wanted and how to get twice the amount out of it. "Dad? Can I go to the video game arcade with Vijay and the guys tomorrow after the game?"

Mr. Jeter raised his eyebrows. "Video game parlor? Is this something new, Derek?"

"Actually it's been there for a while. I've just never been there, and Vij says it's really cool."

"Derek, you know kids sometimes get addicted to those video games," his dad warned.

"But think about it, Dad," Derek said excitedly. "What if I write my paper about that? I could actually do research tomorrow, while I'm playing."

Mr. Jeter looked at Derek skeptically. "Derek. Really? Who are you kidding?"

"No, I mean it, Dad. I really will do a paper, and while I'm playing, I'll be observing how all the other kids are acting, and if they're addicted."

"Well . . . I suppose you could maybe turn it into a semi-educational trip," said Mr. Jeter. "Just don't get carried away with it, that's all."

"Dad, how could you even think I would let that happen?"

"I don't think it. I'm just giving you a heads-up. You can go tomorrow, but only for a couple of hours. No more. Got it?"

"Yesss!" Derek said, breaking into a big smile. "Thanks, Dad. I won't let you down."

"Never mind *me*. If you let anybody down, it'll be yourself, what with finals coming up and this big paper you've got—not to mention baseball."

"I know, I know."

"And oh, by the way, we saw a couple of really nice houses today."

"Dad, I'm tired. Can you tell me about it tomorrow?"

"All right. Lights out then."

"Good night," said Derek, getting into bed.

His dad turned off the light and left the room. Derek lay there in the dark, staring at the ceiling, trying to get the idea of moving out of his brain, so that he could sleep without having bad dreams.

Chapter Eight
THE LIONS' DEN

Everything about today was new. The long ride—almost half an hour. The Lions' field, the stands, and most of all the fact that Derek was playing first base to start the game.

Coach Russell still had him hitting third, at least. That much was the same, as was the entire batting order.

Mason led off with a walk, which was always a good sign. He stole second on the first pitch to Nate, who hit a single on the next pitch, scoring Mason for the first run of the game!

Derek came up to the plate thinking, *All I need is a double to drive Nate in.*

He wasn't trying to do too much; he wasn't trying to

hit it over the fence or anything. Yet he swung through two fastballs that were right over the plate. He couldn't believe he'd missed them *both*.

He was still thinking about it when the pitcher fired a third one right by him, for a called strike three.

Derek tried to keep the sound of his teammates' groans out of his mind, but he knew he'd let them down. How had he missed those pitches? There was nothing especially tricky about them . . . and he'd always been good at hitting fastballs . . .

Harry, at least, managed to hit the ball, a grounder to short that the Lions turned into a double play to end the inning. So the West Siders had to settle for just the one run.

Derek blamed himself for not getting a hit, or at least advancing Nate to second. He still couldn't believe he'd missed those fastballs.

Now he stood at first, pounding his mitt and wishing he had a real first baseman's glove. They were bigger than infielders' gloves and shaped more like a catcher's mitt, made for scooping balls thrown in the dirt by the other infielders.

Mo was pitching today, with Harry playing second. Mo struck out the first batter, and once again Derek got that optimistic feeling. He hopped up and down, staying on the balls of his feet so he'd be ready for any ball that came his way.

The next batter hit a grounder to short. Nate was playing there in place of Derek. He moved to his right to snag it, then fired to first. But the throw was wide, into the onrushing runner.

Derek tried to reach for it while still keeping his foot on the bag. The ball ticked off his mitt, hit the runner on the arm, and skittered into foul territory.

"Ow!" the runner shouted as he took second base, still rubbing the sore spot where Nate's throw had nailed him.

Derek could have kicked himself. He knew he should have forgotten about keeping his foot on the bag so he could catch the ball and prevent the runner from going any farther.

He felt even worse about it when the next batter singled the runner in to tie the score at 1–1. Mo then got a double play to end the frame, but if Derek had kept that runner at first, the Lions wouldn't have scored at all and the West Siders would still have the lead.

They went down one, two, three in the second. Mo returned to the mound, but he seemed to have left his accuracy behind. He walked the first two batters on only nine pitches, and Derek wondered if the game was about to get away from them.

The next hitter smacked a hard grounder to Derek's right. Both Derek and Harry, the second baseman, went for the ball. Derek dived for it and snagged it, but there was no one for him to throw to. Mo was only halfway to first base, and Harry was standing there looking helpless while the Lions cheered and whooped it up at their good fortune.

That ball should have been Harry's, Derek chided himself. *I should have been covering the bag, and we might have had a double play.* Instead it was now bases loaded with nobody out.

Derek told himself to buckle down and pay closer attention to his positioning at first. He was hoping for a triple play, or some other miracle to keep the game close.

But the table had been set for the Lions, and they took full advantage. By the time Mo and the West Siders got through the inning, the score was 5–1 in the home team's favor.

The first two West Siders hitters went down meekly in their half of the third. Then Mason came up and hit a ball over the right fielder's head. By the time the Lions had finished throwing it back in, he'd come all the way around to score the West Siders' second run!

Derek grabbed his bat and got into the on-deck circle, hoping he'd have a chance to get up to the plate this inning and make up for his mistakes. When Nate doubled to left, Derek got his opportunity.

He stood in the batter's box practicing his line drive swing. He was going to get this run in, for sure. On the first pitch he swung right out of his shoes, expecting a fastball but getting a changeup.

"Strike one!" cried the umpire.

Derek told himself to calm down. He took deep breaths, just the way he'd been taught by his dad. Ready to hit again, he stepped back into the box—and stared at strike two.

What had he been looking for? He'd just let a big fat fastball go right by him, without even taking a swing at it.

After a pitch in the dirt allowed Nate to steal third, the pitcher came back with another pitch right down the middle. Derek took aim and put his best swing on it, and hit nothing but air.

"Strike three!" yelled the ump.

Derek couldn't believe it. How had he missed it? In the cages he would have hit that same pitch a hundred times out of a hundred. What in the world was happening to his swing? Was he actually *losing* it?

"Quit overswinging," Coach Russell told him sternly when he got back to the bench. "You're letting your play in the field affect your hitting."

Derek didn't know what to say, but he felt the sting of his coach's words. Not that he hadn't been just as hard on himself. Or maybe that was the problem.

Travel team was not like Little League. The competition here was stiffer, the expectations were higher, and the failures hurt much more. *That's okay,* Derek told himself. *When I do succeed, it'll be that much sweeter.* At least he hoped so.

Coach Russell put him back at shortstop in the bottom of the fourth. Derek felt *much* more comfortable right away. He knew why Coach wanted his players to learn multiple positions, but that didn't mean Derek had to *like* it.

The score was still 5–2, Lions. Harry was now pitching, with Mo having moved to third. Harry struck out the first man, walked the second, struck out the third, and walked the fourth. He was throwing a lot of pitches, and Derek had lots of time out there to stand around waiting in between each pitch.

Coach Russell had told him to get out of his own head. But that didn't help Derek, because he had no idea how to quiet the annoying little voice in his brain. It kept reminding him about those two mistakes he'd made at first base. Even worse, it kept reminding him that something mysterious was wrong with his swing.

Was it that he'd grown four inches? Had that messed up his natural hand-eye coordination or something? Had he lost the skills he'd developed over the years? Would he ever be able to get them back?

CRACK!

Derek came to instant attention. The hitter had just smacked a line drive right at him. Derek held up his mitt to protect his face—and *caught the ball*!

His teammates cheered, and Derek flashed a guilty grin, like the kid who'd been caught raiding the cookie jar.

Well, at least his instincts hadn't deserted him. On

the other hand, he'd been caught daydreaming and had almost paid for it with a bloody nose.

At any rate they'd gotten through the inning without falling any further behind. Now it was time to mount a comeback and win this game.

But the comeback never happened. The Lions' pitchers proved to be too much for the West Siders, who did not score again. And as if the day hadn't gone badly enough, it was Derek who made the last out, foul-tipping it into the catcher's mitt for strike three—his third strikeout of the game, in only three at bats.

The ride home felt longer than the one going to the game. Coach had called a practice for midweek, and Derek knew, having memorized his schedule, that he'd be missing yet another Little League game that day. Just like he had today.

He wondered how the Reds had done without him. He wondered if he'd have had a better time playing in that game instead of this one. *I might have gotten some hits, and it might have been more fun*, he thought.

But he was here to learn, he reminded himself, and to improve his game. And as far as having fun was concerned, Derek knew that for him it all had to do with *winning*. The best way to have fun on this travel team would be to help them win their next game, and the one after that.

Meanwhile, he needed to clear his head of negative

thoughts. He decided to stop rehashing his bad game in his mind, at least for the rest of the day.

Derek smiled as he reminded himself what he was going to be doing that afternoon.

Talk about having fun.

Ding! Ding! Bzzzzz!

The sounds of the video game arcade filled Derek's ears—a symphony of fun as players racked up points, diamonds, coins, and mushrooms. Lights flashed on and off in all different colors.

In the dark arcade, kids' faces were lit up by the lights of the games they sat in front of. None of them were smiling. None looked like they were having fun. All their faces were tense, concentrating on not having their characters die in whatever game they were absorbed in.

To his left Derek spotted Gary Parnell, deep into a game of *Tetris*, manipulating falling blocks before they hit bottom, making them fit the holes in the structure so he could advance to the next level.

To Derek's right, Jeff Jacobson and Harry Hicks were racing cars against each other. One was driving a *Mario* character, the other *Luigi*. They careened around the cartoonlike video racetrack, bombing each other's cars with turtle shells.

Vijay stood in front of another video console. His face glowed, lit up by the reflections of *Super Mario World*.

They were all hypnotized by the colorful, creative worlds in front of them, Derek realized.

Derek thought of his paper on video game addiction. He would have plenty of material to write about, he decided, based on what he was seeing.

After strolling around the arcade, he parked himself in front of a machine offering video baseball, and began feeding tokens into it. . . .

How long have I been at it? Derek wondered after a while. He'd lost track of how long he'd been playing a baseball video game.

There were no clocks on the walls here, unlike at home or in his classroom. It felt like he'd only been playing for twenty minutes or so, but he knew that couldn't be true.

All he knew was, he'd burned through almost all the money he'd brought with him, having gone back to the cashier to buy more tokens several times. It was far more than he'd planned on spending here, but it was too late to change that now. And the game was in the seventh inning, with the score tied. He needed to finish it, even if it cost him a little more to get the victory.

He went back to the cashier, exchanged his last three dollars, and inserted into the machine the tokens he'd gotten. Only when the game was over and he'd lost in the ninth inning did Derek get up and check the time.

He was shocked to see that it was already five o'clock.

His parents were supposed to pick him up at five. Were they already outside?

Derek told Vijay he was going to go check, but he wasn't sure Vijay heard him. Vijay gave no sign but just continued working the knobs and buttons on his *Super Mario World* game. At his feet lay a paper bag half-filled with quarters, so Derek knew his friend wasn't nearly done yet. And Harry's mom wasn't picking up Vijay and the other kids until six.

There was his parents' old brown station wagon, its flashers on in the drizzle that had started just as they'd dropped him off here. He knew they'd been house-hunting in the meantime. He only hoped they hadn't found anything tempting enough to tell him about.

It annoyed him that Sharlee was so enthusiastic about them moving. That made it three against one in the family, and Derek felt she should have been on his side. Where was her loyalty to Mount Royal, anyway? And why didn't his parents spend their money on a new car instead? Their old house was much nicer than their old car.

Across the street Derek saw the building where the batting cages were. Now that he'd spent all his money, he wished he'd gone there instead of the video arcade. He'd thought of it even while he'd been playing, that he could have been working on his swing, to get out of his hitting slump.

But he'd kept on playing, letting himself be totally absorbed by the video version of baseball.

Now his savings were gone and he'd done nothing to improve his swing. He hadn't meant to spend it all in one afternoon. But once he'd gotten into playing the video game, there'd been no stopping. The arcade machine had kept eating his money every new inning, and he'd had to finish the games he'd started, hadn't he?

Except that now he had nothing left for the cages going forward. He'd have to do more chores to make up for that lost money, and when was he going to have time for that? Not anytime soon, that was for sure.

And by the time his birthday rolled around, it would be too late to salvage his batting average for the season.

Chapter Nine

HOUSES AND THE HAUNTED

Looking at houses was creepy, Derek thought. First of all, *other people lived there*. How was that not weird, to be walking through strangers' homes?

Second of all, people decorated and furnished their houses with stuff he and his family would never think of buying. In fact, if someone gave those things to the Jeters as gifts, his family would need to find a way to re-gift the things to someone else!

And where were the people who lived in these places? Why weren't they here? Had they cleared out just so the Jeters could come in and tromp through their house? How was *that* not weird?

"Having fun, old man?" his mom asked, flashing a wry smile.

"Are you kidding?"

"Come on now," his dad interjected. "We're all in this together, Derek. Whichever house we decide to move to will be *all* of ours. It's only right that we should all go looking together."

"But, Dad . . ."

"Derek, quit being a downer," Sharlee said, tugging at his shirt. "Come on, it's fun. Want to go check out the bedrooms? If we move here, I get the big room!"

Derek made a sour face and pulled his shirt free of her grasp.

"Come on, old man," said his mom. "Sharlee's right. We've narrowed our search down to a handful of places, and there's a lot to like about each of them. It's time you got in on the process with the rest of the family."

"And quit making it a trial for the rest of us," said Mr. Jeter. "Your sister's right."

"As usual," Sharlee added with a grin, and even Derek had to smile. There was no resisting Sharlee if she didn't want to be resisted—not in the end. The sooner he gave up giving everyone a hard time, the better it would be for him *and* them.

And so he started to pay closer attention. It was true, each place did have a lot to recommend it . . . but downsides, too. The first one was on a dead-end street, where he could play catch with . . . with whom, exactly? Did any kids even live on this block? Would he even like them, or vice versa?

The house did have four bedrooms, which meant their dad could use one for a home office, instead of the walk-in closet he used now. It also had a two-car garage. "Big enough to put a hitting cage in," his dad commented, giving him a wink.

The worst thing about the house, and the two others they saw that day, was that they were all too far from *home.* Derek thought of all the years they'd lived at Mount Royal. All those days on Jeter's Hill, so many that the other kids had named it after him.

It felt to Derek like his childhood was coming to an end. Soon he'd be thirteen—a teenager, with all the stuff that age group had to deal with. In a little over a year, he'd be going to high school. And on top of that he now had to say goodbye to the only home he'd ever really known.

He managed to keep up his good cheer for the rest of their house tour. But by the time they got home, Derek was feeling cranky again. He snapped at Sharlee a couple of times when she dared to tease him.

Then he felt bad, seeing how he'd hurt her feelings. But at that moment he just couldn't help himself. Why didn't she see that he was going through something, and just leave him alone with his misery?

"Okay, let's have it, old man." His mom stood at his bedroom door, looking across the room at Derek, who lay on his back in bed, staring up at the ceiling. "What's going on with you?"

"Nothing," Derek said, feeling shaky.

"Don't give me that. Come on, who're you kidding? It's *me* here." She gave him a long look, waiting for an answer.

"What?" Derek finally said.

"Since when do you provoke your sister all afternoon and evening?"

"Me?"

"You know you were, Derek. Luckily, Sharlee's in a good mood today. She didn't seem to notice. But you can't hide from me or your dad. So, what's up?"

"Aw, I blew all my money playing video games," he admitted.

"Well, why'd you do that?"

"I don't know. It was so fun while I was playing, but then it felt . . . empty. And when I came outside and saw the cages across the street, I wished I'd spent it on that instead."

"Well, video games are fun because they take our attention away from whatever's bothering us," his mom said. "Of course, in the end, we can't run away from challenges. We have to deal with them."

"And then I'm getting into the car, and Sharlee's like, 'Oh, we saw all these beautiful houses . . .'"

"You making fun of your sister now?"

"No, Mom. But it's just so irritating," he blurted out. "She's so into moving away from here and stuff . . ."

"And so are your father and I," she finished for him.

"Seems to me you're the only one who's not excited."

"Why do we have to move? Don't you guys like it here?"

"We like it very much," she replied. "But you've got to admit, old man, it's gotten smaller as you kids have gotten bigger. Plus your dad really does need a home office."

Derek turned over in bed so he was facing away from her.

"Look, old man, life is change," she went on, coming over and sitting down beside him. "Every day there's a new and different challenge. Things change even when we like them the way they are."

"Mm-hmm," said Derek, not committing one way or the other.

"You've changed too, in case you haven't noticed. You're really getting to be a young man. Am I supposed to complain because you're not going to be my little boy anymore?"

"Aw, Mom," he said. "I'm sorry I've been cranky."

"Well, maybe that's why I call you 'old man.'"

He laughed along with her. "But really, Mom. It's not just about moving. It's like . . . well, Vijay's all into the video game scene like a bunch of my other friends. And he's not into baseball anymore . . . and Dave moved away, and soon I won't even be at Saint Augustine . . ."

"It's a lot to deal with," said his mom. "But life doesn't get any easier. So you have to get stronger and tougher and wiser all the time, so you can deal with all those changes and challenges."

She put a hand on his shoulder. "Don't worry, old man. You can do it. And we'll be right there with you, every step of the way."

She stood back up. "Now get some sleep. And quit worrying about everything. It'll all work itself out. You'll see."

"Even my hitting slump?" he asked.

She cocked her head. "Oh, so *that's* it. I *knew* there was something else. Well, if I spot a flaw in your swing, I'll let you know."

After kissing him on the forehead, she turned off the light and left the room.

Derek lay there in the dark. Finally he fell asleep. He dreamt of failing his finals, striking out to lose the game, and moving to a haunted house. A ghoul was chasing him down the stairs—

He bolted up in bed, about to scream, but thankfully, he stopped himself in time. The last thing he wanted was to have to explain his nightmares to his parents.

Chapter Ten
FIGHTING THROUGH IT

Derek felt a little better after his talk with his mom. Knowing she and Sharlee were in the stands for his travel team game on Wednesday afternoon definitely made him feel more at ease.

Best of all, Coach Russell had him back at shortstop, where, at least in his own mind, he belonged. Before the game started, his mom made her way down to the team bench from the stands.

"Derek!" she called to him, waving for him to come over. "Remember, get out of your own head, and get your head into the game," she urged him. "See the ball, hit the ball. Don't make it any more complicated than that. Okay?"

"Got it," he said, nodding.

"Okay," she said, clapping her hands hard twice. "Go get 'em."

Out there for the top of the first, Derek looked around at his teammates. Everyone was back in their original positions, and that made him feel comfortable too. Derek realized what a creature of habit he'd become—or maybe he always had been.

No time to think about that now, though. Like his mom had said, he needed to get out of his own head and get his head into the game. Derek was determined not to blow this second chance to play the position he loved.

The visiting Braves were big and tall, almost every one of them, except for their leadoff hitter, who looked about nine but hit with surprising power. He launched one over the second baseman's head for a single, and then stole second and third before Harry struck out the next two batters.

The cleanup hitter hit a one-hopper over the mound. Derek and Nate both went for it, but Derek could see he had the better play, because he was running toward first base, not away from it.

"I got it," he shouted. Nate dived out of the way as Derek snagged the ball and fired midstep, to just beat the runner for the out at first, ending the inning and preventing the run from scoring.

"YEAAAH!" he yelled, pounding his mitt as he ran back to the bench. "LET'S GO!"

The West Siders started off well, with a single and a walk. Up came Derek, determined to do something positive at the plate for a change. It had been a while since he'd had a hit. *Now's the time*, he told himself.

But every time he swung, he made no contact. Three swings and he was out, just like that.

The walk back to the bench was agonizing, and Derek avoided Coach Russell's worried gaze.

Harry hit the ball hard at least, but his sharp grounder to short led to a double play to end the first. No score, and on they went to the second inning.

With a man on first and one out, the batter hit a hard line drive to Derek's right. Derek dived and snagged it. Then, seeing that the runner had strayed too far off first, Derek got right back up and fired over there to end the inning.

Another big play for Derek, and it was only the second inning.

When the West Siders came to bat in the bottom of the second, Derek stood behind the chain-link fence, cheering Mo, Brad, and the others as they came to bat. But although the West Siders got two runners on, they failed to score again when Landon swung through a changeup for the third out.

Still no score as they went to the third inning.

Derek grabbed his glove to go back out there. "Head in the game," he muttered to himself. He handled a pop-up and an easy grounder to record the first two outs that inning. But the Braves then hit a triple and a double, to score the first run of the game, before Harry got the third out on a pop-up to second.

Derek knew he was up third this inning. Now more than ever he wanted to contribute at the plate, to get back to being the hitter he'd been all his life.

Mason led off by flying out to center, and Nate struck out swinging, so Derek came up with nobody on base and the home team on the bench looking downcast.

"GO, DEREK!" he heard Sharlee shout as he stepped into the batter's box. Even in a big crowd he could always make out her distinctive voice. He looked over and waved. She waved back, and so did her friends, the Parker triplets. The four of them were jumping up and down in the stands.

Derek looked away and got his head back into the game. He pulled his batting helmet down over his forehead and raised the bat over his shoulder. *Ready . . .*

He kept his eye on the ball and put his best swing on it—but instead of hitting it on the sweet spot of the bat and launching the ball, he missed by a quarter of an inch and popped it straight up into the air.

Derek ran to first for all he was worth, hoping the catcher would drop the ball. But he caught it easily, and Derek made the slow walk back to the bench hanging his head in frustration and disappointment.

Half the game gone, and they were still down by a run.

Mo took over from Harry on the mound. He was a differ-ent kind of pitcher than Harry. They both threw fastballs, but Mo was tall and threw almost sidearm, whipping the ball toward the plate. Hitters would jump out of the way for perfect strikes, fooled by the movement on the ball.

Mo struck out the side in the fourth, and the score stayed 1–0.

Derek watched again from the bench as the middle of the West Siders' order went down one, two, three.

The game couldn't go on like this, Derek sensed. Sooner or later one team was going to break through. He sure hoped it was *his* team.

Mo got in trouble with one out in the fifth, walking two batters and giving up a run-scoring single before steady-ing himself and striking out the final two hitters. But now it was 2-0 Braves, and time was running out for the West Siders to come back.

If this had been Little League, the bottom of the order would have been made up of kids who couldn't hit very well. But on the travel league it was different. All these kids could hit. And the Braves had now put in a relief pitcher who wasn't nearly as accurate or overpowering.

Daxon got the team started in the bottom of the fifth with a clean single to left. Christian quickly doubled him home, and the deficit was cut in half, just like that.

Landon singled home the tying run, and Derek could

feel the excitement of the comeback coursing through his veins. Everyone was yelling and whooping as Mason stepped to the plate.

But Mason overswung. He hit a dribbler back to the pitcher, who threw to second to get the lead runner. Then the second baseman fired to first, just ahead of Mason, who had good speed but had swung so hard that he'd lost his balance and gotten a slow start.

Nate came up with the bases empty and was clearly trying to hit one to the moon. He took big swings, but in the end he grounded out meekly to first to end the inning.

At least the game was tied now. It was up to the West Siders defense to hold the score where it was so they could walk it off in the sixth. Derek knew he'd be leading off next inning. He was determined to help his team score, no matter what. But if they didn't hold the Braves here, it might not even matter.

"Hit it right here," Derek said under his breath, bouncing up and down on the balls of his feet.

As if in answer the hitter popped one over Derek's head. He ran back on it, sure he had it the whole time. At the last second, though, he stubbed his toe on a tuft of grass. He somehow managed to grab the ball in the middle of doing a somersault in short left field!

One out, and Derek basked in the sound of cheers from the home team's stands.

Mo got the next two hitters on strikeouts, and the West

Siders ran back to the bench, buzzing with excitement.

"Nice play, Derek!" they all told him, clapping him on the back and helmet.

"Let's go!" they called after him as he strode to the plate.

Derek let the first pitch go by. Ball one.

And that was his fastball, he thought, unimpressed. But somehow when he swung at the next pitch, he made no contact. *Again.*

It sent chills through him. He'd tracked that ball all the way. At least he thought he had. How had he missed it?

Timing, he realized. The pitcher's changes of speed were throwing him off, just like the rest of the West Siders. He tried again to put bat on ball, and fouled it off behind home plate.

Two strikes now . . . and suddenly Derek had an idea. If he couldn't hit this kid—and it was clear to him that as things stood, he couldn't—then he could still do *something* to help his team win. Even with two strikes, he could *bunt*.

It would be the last thing the Braves expected. If you foul off a bunt with two strikes, you're out, so it almost never happens. But Derek had noticed that all the infielders were playing him deep. All he had to do was make soft contact and lay the bunt down in fair territory.

Here came the pitch, slower than slow. Derek squared around and pushed the bunt up the third-base line.

Stay fair! Stay fair! he thought, not looking as he ran to first with everything he had.

"Safe!" said the umpire as Derek crossed ahead of the stunned third baseman's throw.

"LET'S GO!" he yelled to his teammates, clapping his hands fiercely.

Harry let the first three pitches go by, giving Derek a chance to steal second. On the third one, a changeup, Derek went. He slid in easily, way ahead of the throw from the Braves' frustrated catcher.

Harry then grounded out to second, with Derek advancing to third with only one out. Just a fly ball from Mo, and Derek would score the winning run.

But Mo struck out. Now there were two gone. It was up to Brad—and he came through for the team with a ground ball that found a hole between the first and second basemen.

Derek ran home and was mobbed by his ecstatic teammates. Final score, 3–2, West Siders!

After the celebration Derek found his way into the stands, where he high-fived his mom and Sharlee, and of course the Parker triplets had to high-five him too. He was happy to oblige them. After all, his team was now 2–1 and he'd been a big part of the victory. True, he still wasn't hitting well, but he'd think about that tomorrow. For now he wanted to enjoy the win.

"Some great stuff out there in the field, old man," his

mom said proudly. "Don't worry about the hitting. It'll come around."

She'd meant to sound encouraging, but her words only made Derek realize how obvious his poor hitting had been. If his mom had noticed, surely the coach had too. . . .

"Derek." Coach Russell was motioning him over. "Nice game today," he told Derek, giving him five and smiling. "I guess you've made your case to play shortstop."

"Thanks, Coach." Those were just the words he'd wanted to hear.

"Say, listen," the coach went on, "any chance you might have some extra time between now and Saturday afternoon to work on that swing of yours?"

Derek felt his heart drop into his cleats. "Uh, I don't know, Coach," he said. "I will have to ask my mom or dad. But I've got a Little League game Saturday morning too, so I can work on it then."

Coach Russell frowned. "Well, I'd rather you were doing it with a coach around. Or at least your dad. He's coached before, hasn't he?"

"Uh-huh."

"I think it'd really do you a lot of good," said the coach. "You've got a great swing, but it's just . . . off a little somehow. Not *far* off. You just need reps. Try to get to the cages if you can, and find your old swing again, okay?"

"Sure, Coach," Derek said, not at all sure that his parents would be able to take him. They were busier than usual, what with house-hunting. Besides, he'd blown all his own savings on video games. Would they be willing to foot the bill for him to spend extra time in the cages, when he'd just spent his own money so foolishly?

"In the meantime," Coach Russell concluded, "I'm dropping you down to seventh in the order. Just for next game. You understand. As soon as you get back to hitting like yourself, we'll get you back up there in the order."

Derek was ultra-quiet on the way home. He knew Coach Russell was just being practical. Still, it really, really hurt.

And as for his swing, would he *ever* get it back?

Chapter Eleven

DOING THE WORK

Derek was working away at the opening pages of his report on video game addiction when his dad appeared in the doorway of his bedroom. "Nice," he said approvingly, seeing Derek hard at work. "Glad to see you aren't putting things off till the last minute."

"It's hard, though," Derek admitted. "It's tough slogging through all this material. And I'm trying to use Vijay and Jeff and Harry and the other kids as examples, so there's a lot."

"Well, keep at it. You seem like you're onto something good there. And don't get discouraged if it's slow going. Challenges are good for us. They help us push our limits."

"Dad," Derek said, looking up from his work, "I really

need you to take me to the cages. My hitting's gone totally south."

"First of all," said his dad, coming over to him, "your hitting will be just fine. You need to work out some mechanical things, your timing, get your head back in the right place—"

"Well, I need you to help me! Please, Dad. It's an emergency. I've got two games on Saturday, and I don't want to strike out ten times."

"Your mom tells me you spent all your money at that video game parlor last weekend. Was that wise?"

"Dad, I know I messed up. I wasn't going to spend it all, just *part* of it. But then when I was done, there wasn't any money left. I don't even know how that happened. It was just . . . the game kept needing more if I wanted to keep on playing, and—"

"Well, write about it in that paper you're doing. Treat yourself as subject number one."

"Dad. Please. I'll do chores to make up for the money, I promise!"

"And when will you have time to do chores?"

"Um . . . over the summer?" Derek suggested. "Anyway, my birthday's coming up. Someone's bound to give me money as a present, enough for a session at the cages. If you loan me enough money now, I can pay you back then."

Mr. Jeter considered this. "All right, Derek, I'll tell you what. If you work on your paper the rest of this evening, and tomorrow as well, I'll take you after school on Friday. Mom's and my treat."

"Yessss!" Derek said excitedly. "Thank you, Dad. Thank you, thank you, thank you!"

"All right, all right. Now get back to work. I'm going to need to look over your progress before I take you anywhere."

Derek got back to work, but now he had a smile on his face. Things were looking up.

"You're lunging at it, Derek." His dad paused the pitching machine and pantomimed the way Derek was swinging. "See how my whole body is sliding forward? That's not how you want to do it. Stay back, and don't open up your hips too soon. Let the ball come to you. Now, let's try it again."

It was amazing to Derek how his dad could always spot the flaws in his game. Mr. Jeter had been a really good baseball player in college, and only an injury to his knee and an inability to hit the curveball had forced him to quit playing competitively.

But he could still share everything he knew with his children, and he did. Both Derek and Sharlee were benefitting. Sharlee stood there watching now, impatiently waiting for her turn in the cage.

"Daddy, when do I get to hit?" she piped up.

"Soon, Sharlee. We've got to fix Derek's swing first."

"What about my swing?"

"Your swing? Your swing is perfect," said her dad with a smile.

"Daddy!" said Sharlee, stomping her foot. Derek had to smile. Sharlee wasn't shy about her abilities, but at least she knew her game wasn't perfect.

This round, Derek tried consciously to stay back, with his weight on his right foot, bat pulled back so his left arm grazed his chin. He hit a bunch of balls the other way, all solidly.

"That's the stuff," said his dad, clapping. "Try to go the other way or up the middle. Don't try to pull anything. You'll end up pulling the slow pitches anyway."

Derek hit and hit, until his hands hurt, then sat down to watch Sharlee take her turn. He had to admit he was impressed. His little sister could seriously hit. She looked and acted like a pro ballplayer.

"Whose stance is that you're copying?" Derek teased her.

"Yours, silly," she said, throwing it right back at him, giving as good as she got. Derek laughed and shook his head. Was there ever a better little sister than his?

By the end of the session, all three of them were exhausted. "I hope you're not too tired to hit tomorrow," Mr. Jeter told them both. "Derek, you've got a double-header, right?"

"Little League at ten, travel team at two," he said, having memorized it from his calendar.

"Wow," said Mr. Jeter. "We'd better pack you some snacks."

"Can you come to the travel game, Dad?" Derek pleaded with him. "Sharlee's game will be over by then."

"I'll be there. You, Sharlee?"

"YAY!" Sharlee said, clapping her hands. "A whole day of baseball!"

Derek was lying in bed, trying to get to sleep, when his dad poked his head around the bedroom door. "You still awake?"

"Uh-huh."

"Good." His dad came in and sat down on the bed next to him.

"Let's talk a little more about your hitting."

"More? I thought we fixed everything back there in the cages."

"Mmm, not entirely. I want to talk with you about what's going on in your head while you're up at the plate."

"Oh. Okay. Like what?"

"That's what I'm wondering. Because all the stuff we worked on today you already knew. You used to do it all automatically. I know you're four inches taller now, and your body's different, but fixing those mechanics is the easy part. I think you got into this slump of yours by not paying attention to your mental game."

"My mental game?"

"That's right. You've got to have a clear mind up there at the plate. You can't be wondering if you're good enough to be on the team, or thinking about the error you made last inning, or showing your coach you're a great hitter—none of that."

"Yeah," Derek agreed. "Mom said it: 'See the ball, hit the ball.'"

"That's right. If you've got too many things buzzing around in your mind, it's tough to focus. Got to lose whatever's getting in the way."

"Thanks, Dad. I'll think about it."

"Good boy. And go get 'em tomorrow. Both games."

He hugged Derek and went downstairs. Derek settled into bed, staring at the dark ceiling. His focus had been all over the place, and he knew it. Thinking about two different baseball teams, school, Vijay, addictions . . .

And *video games*. How many times in the past couple of weeks had Derek's mind wandered back to *Super Mario World*, or some other cartoonlike video world? Lots.

He'd had a hard lesson at the arcade that day, but ever since then, every day at school Vijay had been talking about video games—and so had all the other kids. It was like if you weren't talking about video games, Vijay wasn't interested—and neither was Jeff, Harry, or even Gary Parnell.

Vijay had asked Derek three days in a row if he wanted to come over and play video games. Derek had turned him down each time, reluctantly. He had to work on his paper, after all, and go to the cages before his hitting slump became a permanent feature.

But that didn't mean he wasn't *thinking* about video games. Video games were on his mind dozens of times every day, because that's what he was writing about in his paper.

He couldn't wait till the assignment was done. If he couldn't stop thinking about video games by then, he'd know he was truly addicted.

As for Vijay, Derek was really worried. He'd already lost one best friend when Dave had moved to Hong Kong with his family. Now Vijay had quit baseball and was totally into video games. Derek could definitely feel him drifting away as well.

But Vijay or no Vijay, Derek knew that if he wanted to keep his baseball dreams alive, he couldn't let little things like video games distract *him*.

Chapter Twelve

DOUBLEHEADER!

Derek showed up on Saturday for his Little League game, and right away he felt weird. He'd gotten used to being on the travel team, to throwing himself totally into that world. Being back here in his old league was jarring.

He barely remembered most of his teammates, and a few of them seemed surprised to see him.

"I thought he quit the team," Derek heard Charlie whisper to Zeke.

Still, they seemed glad to have him back. He'd helped them win that first game of the season. He felt a little embarrassed that he'd barely shown up since.

Derek felt bad about that, but he really didn't see how he could have done anything differently, other than not play Little League at all. And how would that have helped them?

He was grateful that they didn't hold it against him, and he promised himself he'd do something today to help them win this one too. They sure needed it. In his absence the Reds had lost four in a row and now had a 1–4 record.

Derek told himself to stay in the moment, not to let his mind chew over what might have been or what wasn't going to be. The only things he could change were right here, right now.

Today they were the visiting team. As in his previous Little League game, Derek was slated into the cleanup spot. Derek didn't get up in the first inning, though, because George, Charlie, and Zeke all went down swinging.

"This pitcher's too tough," said Charlie as he lay down his bat and grabbed his mitt.

Derek sure hoped that wasn't true. In any case he wasn't about to let it shake him. Going to the cages with his dad had left him feeling calmer and more confident about his hitting.

He was kept busy at short. Zeke induced three ground-outs, and all of them came Derek's way. Derek handled them effortlessly, then jogged back to the bench, grabbed a helmet and his bat, and strode to the plate. He took a few vicious practice swings, just so the pitcher could see his intentions. *Let* him *be the one who's nervous,* Derek told himself.

He let two pitches go by, both balls. *Good,* thought Derek. *Now he has to throw this one over the plate.*

The pitch was a strike, and Derek swung. He hit the top half of the ball, well enough that the resulting grounder scooted past the second baseman for a hit. The Reds all cheered, excited to see that the Cubs' pitcher was not Superman.

That seemed to inspire Ernesto, the Reds' next hitter. He singled up the middle, sending Derek to third. Elliott managed a fly ball to center, and Derek scored on the play to make it 1–0. Norman then struck out, and Ben popped out to end the inning, but at least they had a lead.

Out at shortstop Derek reflected on his first at bat. He'd swung too hard, letting his excitement get the better of him. If he'd kept his cool, he could have hit that ball a lot better, he knew. Next time he would, he promised himself.

Zeke was pitching well, or else the Cubs' hitters weren't that good. Derek couldn't tell which—maybe a combination of the two. The next inning and a half went by in a flash, with neither team able to muster any runs, or even hits or walks.

In the top of the fourth, Zeke led off with a double down the right field line. Derek came to the plate, laser-focused on driving him in.

The first pitch was in the dirt, and the ball got away from the catcher. Zeke made it to third easily. On the second pitch Derek was ready. The pitch was a fastball, but Derek had seen much faster pitches while he was playing travel ball, and this one was straight over the heart of the plate.

Derek sent the ball sailing deep to left, over the outfielder's head. Zeke jogged home, admiring the ball's flight along with everyone else.

Derek took nothing for granted, though. He kept running full speed, turning what would have been a triple into an inside-the-park home run!

Now it was 3–0, Reds. The Cubs switched pitchers, but it didn't help. The rout was officially on. By the time the game was over, the Reds had notched their second victory of the season, with a score of 8–2.

Derek wound up going 4 for 4, adding a double and another single. He played short the whole game and made a couple of outstanding plays to top off his excellent offensive game.

Everybody congratulated him. All the Reds were happy to have broken their losing streak, and there was no doubt that Derek, along with Zeke, had been the biggest contributors to the victory.

"So," Charlie said to him afterward, "when are we going to see you again?"

"Um, I don't know," Derek replied. "I'll have to check my calendar."

Charlie scowled. "Oh. Right. Your calendar. Well, thanks for stopping by." He turned and walked away, and Derek could tell he was mad.

Derek felt a surge of guilt go through him, but he shook it off. What was he supposed to do, other than showing up when he could and doing his best?

He didn't let the feeling linger, instead going over to his mom and walking back to the car with her. They needed to get home so Derek could have lunch before this afternoon's travel game.

By the time he'd finished eating and he, his dad, and Sharlee were in the car, Derek had banished all thoughts of that morning's game from his mind. He needed to focus on the game to come.

But his dad wasn't done talking about it. "Your mom says your swing looked fine," he said. "You remembered all the stuff we went over?"

"Uh-huh."

"Well, batting a thousand this morning is pretty good. But you know the pitchers in travel league are much tougher."

In fact, Derek was concerned about that very thing. It had all seemed so easy this morning, playing against lesser competition.

"Just remember when you're up there at the plate—try to shoot it up the middle. Don't try to do too much. Stay within yourself. Same swing, level through the hitting zone."

Well, Derek thought, he could take it two ways. Either he could ride the good feelings from this morning's contest, or he could worry that it didn't mean a thing because the pitching had been easy to hit.

No, he thought. *Not going to go there. My swing is back, and that's what counts.*

In contrast to the game that morning, Derek felt totally comfortable back on the field with the West Siders. Coach Russell had him at short for infield practice. But when the lineup was announced, Derek was listed as seventh in the batting order, just as Coach had said he would be.

Derek felt ashamed. He imagined that all the other kids on the team were feeling sorry for him.

Well, he'd have to turn that around in a hurry.

But he couldn't very well hurry while hitting seventh in the order. He might not even get up to bat until the third inning.

The West Siders started out in the field, and the leadoff man for the South Side Orioles came up to bat.

Stay in the moment, Derek told himself. *Don't be thinking about hitting now. Take it one challenge at a time. . . .*

Harry started off by giving up a screaming double to left. The second batter hit it on the nose. Derek saw it coming for him, veering right toward his face at what felt like a zillion miles an hour.

He flinched, stuck his glove out to protect his face—and caught the ball. "Oww!" he yelled as the stinging pain penetrated his palm.

But he didn't lose focus. Seeing that the runner had strayed too far off second, he fired over there, and Nate nailed the tag to complete the double play.

All the West Siders cheered but none more than Harry, who certainly looked relieved. Two out, nobody on, instead of a run in and a man on first with no outs.

Harry responded with an inspired strikeout to end the top of the first, and now it was the West Siders' turn to try to do some damage.

Derek had to sit and watch as his team mounted an immediate threat. Mason walked, then Nate doubled him over to third. Harry, batting in the spot where Derek would have normally hit, struck out. Derek wished it had been him up there. He couldn't help feeling he would have knocked those runs in.

Well, they had two more outs, so maybe things would work out after all, he thought. And when Mo walked to load the bases, things were looking promising for sure.

But Brad lined out to third base, freezing the runners in place. And Daxon's long fly ball was run down by the center fielder for the third out. Derek groaned along with the rest of the West Siders. Bases loaded, one out, and no runs scored.

Derek was even more upset than the rest of his teammates. If only he'd been batting higher in the order—even sixth—he *knew* he could have done the job. But of course he'd put himself into this position by getting into a hitting slump.

Still, no time to think about that now. Back in the field he had to help keep this game scoreless.

Harry walked the first two men he faced, before striking out the third. The next man hit it hard to Derek's right. He dived, snagged it, and then flipped it to Brad at third for the second out. Brad fired to first, just ahead of the runner, to end the inning on the pitcher's best friend—a double play, and a sparkler at that.

Now, finally, it was Derek's turn to hit. This was the most important at bat he'd had in a long time. Not because of the game situation but because he had so much to prove to his coaches and teammates—and even more, to *himself.*

He blew out a few deep breaths and stepped into the box. When the pitch came, it looked hittable. He swung so hard that he nearly came out of his shoes.

"Strike one!" called the umpire.

Derek felt a surge of embarrassment shoot through him. He hoped his face didn't look as red as it felt.

When the next pitch came, he wanted to make sure he made solid contact. But he had so much energy surging through his body that he couldn't stay back. Lunging forward, he swung wildly, and missed again.

"Strike two!"

Life is a daily challenge, Derek repeated to himself, remembering what his parents had told him. *This is just one more.*

He told himself to calm down, and his heart to beat more slowly. He twice stepped out of the box, calling time and taking some deep breaths to steady himself. Finally, when he felt focused, he stepped back in.

"Let's go!" shouted one of the Orioles fielders. "We don't have all day."

Derek ignored the catcalling, his eyes on the pitcher's throwing hand. Derek kept his weight back, letting the pitch come to him. Then he swung—and blooped one the other way, just over the second baseman's head, for a single.

His teammates clapped and cheered, but Derek wasn't thrilled. He'd meant to hit a long ball—a double at least—just to show that his swing was back for good.

But although he'd pretty much missed that pitch, here he was on first base, in position to do something good for his team, even if he couldn't hit a baseball to save his life.

Christian took the first two pitches thrown to him. Derek stole second base on the first pitch, and third base on the second pitch. When Christian grounded slowly to short, Derek scored on the play for the game's first run, while Christian beat it out for a single!

Landon struck out, and so did Mason. But Nate and Harry both singled, driving in the team's second run, before Mo lined out to end the inning.

Now it was 2–0, West Siders. Harry, though, was having trouble with his control. After walking two in the second, he now walked two more in the third, and then hit a batter to load the bases with nobody out. Coach Russell called time and came out to the mound to calm Harry down.

Harry hasn't been out on the Hill all season, Derek reflected. He'd been hanging out at the video arcade instead.

Baseball took a lot of focus, Derek had come to understand. And the better the competition, the more focus was needed. Practice, practice, practice, work, work, work— and love every minute of it. That was the only way to achieve his ultimate dream, and he knew it.

He focused back on the game as Coach Russell returned to the bench. Harry threw it over the plate this time, but the Orioles hitter cleared the bases with a double to left.

There went the West Siders' lead. They were now down 3–2, and before the inning was over, it was 5–2, with Mo replacing Harry on the mound for the final out.

In the bottom of the third, Brad led off with a single. Daxon got him over to second on a groundout to first, and it was Derek's turn at bat again, this time with an RBI opportunity.

He was careful not to swing at balls off the plate or up in his eyes. Nor did he swing at the two pitches in the dirt. In the end he walked on five pitches. The one strike he'd been thrown, he hadn't swung at.

As Derek stood on first base, he felt hugely disappointed. He'd meant to drive Brad in from second, but the pitcher hadn't given him anything to hit. The one pitch that had been called a strike had been below his knees, but the ump had called it anyway.

Well, he told himself, *you took what he gave you.* He knew he'd done the right thing, and now here he was on first, with Brad on second and only one out.

On the other hand Derek hadn't done anything yet to impress Coach Russell or convince him to move Derek up in the batting order for the next game.

Christian flew out to center. Brad, after tagging up, took off for third and made it easily when the throw from the center fielder went to second base. Derek held up at first.

Landon got the count to three balls and a strike, then hit a dribbler down the third-base line. Brad had to hold or he would have been tagged out by the third baseman, but Derek was off and running for second. The third baseman, confused what to do with the ball, simply held it, and the bases were loaded.

Now it was back to the top of the order. Mason swung for the fences on the first pitch—and popped it up behind first base. The first and second basemen both went after it. By the time it dropped between them, Brad had already crossed the plate, Derek went to third, and Landon slid safely into second.

Nate came up to hit. When he singled up the middle, Derek and Landon both scored to tie the game at 5–5!

Harry struck out to end the frame, but the West Siders

were psyched now. Derek could feel it too—the strong sense that they were going to win this game.

In the top of the fourth, Mo set the side down in order, striking out two of the three men he faced. Derek was impressed. Where had that curveball come from? It was the first time he'd seen Mo use it, and the Orioles looked like they were surprised too. The only contact made was an easy one-hopper back to the mound. Mo tossed it underhand to first like it was a bouquet of flowers, and that was that.

He's been working on his pitching game, Derek said to himself. *Not like Harry . . .*

In their half of the inning, the West Siders had Daxon on first with two men out when Derek came to the plate for the third time. Derek took two pitches, which gave Daxon time to steal second when the ball got away from the catcher.

Then Derek hit a sharp ground ball that got between the first and second basemen and skittered into right field. He pulled up at first with a single, then watched Daxon slide home safely to put the West Siders ahead, 6–5!

Derek felt a lot better now. It had only been a grounder, of course. If it hadn't been placed perfectly, it would have been an out. Instead he now had himself an RBI, to go with his run scored earlier in the game.

Not a bad day at the plate, even if it wasn't a great one. He hoped the coach thought so, anyway.

Christian flew out to center to end the inning, and it was on to the fifth. Mo continued to dazzle the Orioles hitters, who managed a single and a walk but no more.

In the bottom of the fifth, the West Siders went down one, two, three, and now it was last licks for the Orioles, with the West Siders holding a fragile one-run edge.

Mo stayed out there on the mound for the sixth. But his arm must have been getting tired, or else the Orioles had figured out his curveball, because the first two hitters came through with clean singles.

After a mound visit from the coach, Mo buckled down and got the next two hitters, one on a strikeout and the other on a foul pop-up near first. Now the Orioles were down to their final out.

Derek got into his ready crouch, bouncing on the balls of his feet. On the 2–2 count the hitter lofted a soft fly ball over Derek's head.

He raced back, trying to keep the ball in view over his right shoulder as he ran. It was veering left, and he had to bend his body that way, changing course. He reached out at the last second to grab it for the final out of the game!

With two outs, the runners had been going on contact. Both had already crossed home plate. They went from celebrating one second to groaning in disappointment the next. They'd been sure their team was back in the lead, and suddenly the game was over and they'd lost. All because of a great play by the West Siders' shortstop.

Derek beamed as he accepted his teammates' congratulations. He took off his cap and waved it at his dad and Sharlee, who were on their feet in the stands, clapping.

"Great work in the field today!" Coach Russell said, shaking Derek's hand.

"Thanks, Coach! And . . . at the plate?"

Coach Russell looked at him, then thought about it. "Better," he said. "Coming along. Keep working at it, huh?" He clapped Derek on the shoulder and went off to high-five the rest of the team.

Better . . . Coming along . . . Keep working at it . . .

Well, that was better than nothing, Derek thought, slightly disappointed.

Still, what had he expected, raves? True, he'd gone 2 for 2 with a walk, an RBI, and a run scored. But he'd made only weak contact.

Coach Russell is right, he thought. *I need to keep working on it.*

Chapter Thirteen
CLOSE TO HOME

Sunday morning it rained hard. Derek found it difficult to get out of bed because the sky was so dark that it felt like nighttime. He had breakfast and put in another hour on his term paper, which was shaping up nicely.

He'd included his own personal history with video games—the temptation he'd felt right away to keep on playing, the way he would forget everything else except the fantasy world of the game, the way he would lose track of time. He'd even written about the way he'd squandered all the money he'd saved up, blowing it all at the video game arcade instead of spending it on the thing he really wanted—hitting practice.

His paper also told about the kids Derek knew who

were more seriously into gaming than he had ever been. Of course, he changed their names in the paper so that Mr. Laithwaite wouldn't know who they were. But he'd included Jeff, Gary, Harry, and, of course, Vijay, among others.

Just as Derek was writing a few last things about "Mr. V"—his code name for Vijay—the phone rang.

His mother answered it in the kitchen, then called up the stairs to Derek. "It's Vijay for you."

Derek ran down to the kitchen and took the phone from her. "Hi, Vij!"

"Derek! Want to come over and play *Mario Brothers*?"

Derek told his mom what Vijay had just said. "Can I, Mom?"

She looked at her husband, who was sitting at the table. He shrugged and said, "The boy's been working hard on his paper, Dot. I don't see why not."

"All right, then, old man," she told Derek. "Be back by lunch, though. Your dad and I have narrowed it down to two possible houses. We want you to come see both of them with us this afternoon and help us decide which one to go after."

Derek wasn't thrilled about that part, but he understood. If his parents were down to two houses, that meant he only had to say which one he hated *less*, and that would be the last time they'd bother him for his opinion about moving. That is, until they actually *moved. Ugh.*

Derek didn't want to think about it. At that moment the idea of losing himself in *Super Mario World* was very appealing.

When he got there, Vijay was already absorbed in whatever high level he was on—way past any Derek had ever played, that was for sure.

"Check out this secret pipe," Vijay enthused without ever taking his eyes off the TV screen.

Derek watched as Mario banged a box with his head and a giant vine grew out of the box, twisting toward the sky. Mario climbed it, yelling "woo-hoo," and dived down a pipe that was hanging in midair. It lowered him to a secret room where he collected tons of coins that made the ringing sound of a cash register every time.

"Man, I'm rich!" Vijay cried out in sheer ecstasy as he made Mario leap over a pit of lava and grab the flag at the end of the level. "Here, let me save the game, and then you can have a turn."

Derek had been standing there watching for the past three or four minutes. He couldn't help noticing that Vijay had looked hypnotized the whole time. Something about his old friend had changed from playing so many hours of video games. His eyes seemed glazed over, and all his thoughts were about the virtual world, not the real one.

Derek enjoyed playing *Mario Brothers*, but he definitely didn't want to get into it like Vijay. He didn't want game playing to change who he was, or what he thought was important.

As Derek tried and failed, over and over again, to beat the much easier level his Luigi was on, he realized that his reflections on "Mr. V" needed an update.

"How're you doing on your paper?" he asked Vijay in a casual tone while jumping over a series of bricks and avoiding toxic turtles.

"Oh, that," Vijay said. "To tell you the truth, I haven't gotten very far."

"It's due pretty soon."

"Not that soon," Vijay countered. "More than a week, right?"

"Yeah, by one day. So, how far have you actually gotten?"

"Um, I've been playing with the outline."

"Seriously?" Derek put down the controller, and his Luigi immediately got crushed by a block of bricks. "Dude!"

"I know, I know," Vijay said. "I've got it handled, don't worry."

Derek cocked his head. "Okay, if you say so."

He knew Vijay had always been an A student. He was perfectly capable of writing a six-page paper in less time than Derek himself would have taken. Still, he had to wonder if "Mr. V" really did have things under control as much as he believed he did. This was seventh grade, after all. And Mr. Laithwaite was a notoriously tough grader of papers.

"So, how are you doing on your paper?" Derek asked.

Vijay sighed. "Do we have to talk about it?"

"Well, not really, but—"

"I haven't actually started writing yet, okay? It's just—I keep thinking I'll start it one way, but then I think I want to do it another way . . ."

"Listen, do you want to talk about it? Because I could help you get it started, at least. I know a thing or two about eating sugar."

"And what's *your* topic?" Vijay asked.

"Video game addiction."

"Oh wow. That's a good one!" Vijay laughed out loud. "I hope you talk all about Gary Parnell. He's gone completely ape over video games. Did you notice?"

Derek slowly shook his head in disbelief. Was Vijay so unaware of his *own* addiction to video games?

And what about me? Derek had to ask himself. *Am I really that immune?*

"I don't feel like doing schoolwork this morning," Vijay said, taking the controller back. "It's Sunday, right? I've got the whole week to deal with that paper. Remember, I don't have any ball games or practices to worry about. I've got plenty of time still."

Whatever, thought Derek as he watched Vijay defeat boss after nasty boss. *I sure hope he's right.*

Derek didn't like the real estate agent. His hair was glued down by some kind of spray that smelled really bad, and that filled the office air with fumes that made Derek feel sick.

It was still raining, but not as hard as in the morning. The first house they visited was on a two-way street that seemed busy to Derek. The house itself was big, for sure. His parents and Sharlee kept oohing and aahing about this or that feature the agent showed them. Meanwhile, Derek wandered off by himself to explore the place.

It was what people called a split-level. There were stairs everywhere, although not very many at once. Not like at Mount Royal, where they had one proper set of stairs between the lower and upper floors.

Derek looked at the bedrooms. One was big and really nice. Derek figured that would be for his parents. There were two smaller ones, one of which had its own bathroom. Sharlee would want that one, he knew—and what if he did too?

The backyard was big and level and fenced. "Great for playing catch," his dad pointed out.

Big whoop, thought Derek glumly. *Give me the Hill any day.*

"Well, what did you think?" his mom asked him as they got into the back seat of the car with Sharlee.

"Let's see the other one," Derek replied flatly.

His mom didn't press the point. The second house was much older, but Derek could see right away why his parents liked it. First of all it was on a quiet, tree-lined street near where his dad worked and not far from his mom's accounting agency.

The house itself was a bit worn down, but it had lots of charm. Then Derek saw the bedrooms. All four of them were big, and three had bathrooms of their own. There was even a full playroom in the basement, with a foosball game and a Ping-Pong table set up!

"They belong to the owner, and he's willing to leave them here for you if we like," the agent told them.

"Wow, that's cool," said Derek's mom, trying to get him excited about moving.

But Derek wasn't having any of it. Neither of these places was as good as their townhouse at Mount Royal. Why did they have to move at all?

"So, just give me a call and let me know which one you want to rent," said the agent as they said goodbye outside his office.

The Jeters shook his hand, and got back into their old brown station wagon for the trip back home. The rain had finally stopped, or they would have gotten wet, standing there talking. But as it was, Derek had no excuse to rush them away from their chitchat with the agent.

Finally they were on their way back home. Neither his father nor his mother asked him any questions, clearly sensing his mood, which was dismal.

He knew they'd be moving soon, away from everything he loved about Mount Royal. Although, really, what was left for him there? Vijay, Harry, and Jeff were all only interested in video games, and Derek had firmly made up his mind not to get too into gaming the way they all had.

Besides, he was getting kind of big to play ball on the Hill anyway, with its tree stumps for bases and flat stones for the mound and plate, its sloping outfield where all balls eventually came back down toward the infield . . .

He was going to miss it all. His whole entire childhood was flashing by him when suddenly his mom hit the brakes.

"Look, Jeter!" she said, pointing across the quiet street. There stood a crudely painted wooden sign, reading FOR SALE OR RENT BY OWNER.

"Hey, you know what?" Mr. Jeter replied. "I'll bet that house backs right up to Kalamazoo Central High's athletic fields."

That made Derek sit up and take notice. "The athletic fields?"

"Isn't that the school you're going to in ninth grade?" Sharlee asked him.

"It is," Derek said.

"Here, pull over, Dot, and let me go check," said Mr. Jeter.

"Wait! I'll come with you," Derek said, opening the rear door and hopping out.

"I'm staying here," Sharlee said. "I like the other houses better. This one's yellow, and the lawn is yucky."

Derek didn't think the yellow color was so bad, although the lawn was overgrown for sure.

"The owner probably moved out already," said Mr. Jeter as he and Derek crossed the quiet street and walked up the driveway of the house.

It was the kind called a "bi-level," a term Derek was already familiar with from the real estate agent. The house was on a hill, so there was a lower level that gave access to the fenced backyard. Beyond the fence was a flat expanse of green containing two baseball fields as well as a football field, and beyond that the redbrick school building itself.

The backyard looked down on home plate and the backstop fence. The home team bench was just beyond that, and the visiting bench backed right up to the house's back fence. "We could watch all the games from here!" Derek said, awestruck.

"And when you go to high school, this is where you'll be playing your home games," his dad pointed out. "Short trip back home after, huh? We could clear us a path right down this hill to the field."

"And look there, Dad," said Derek, pointing to a full tub of baseballs sitting near home plate.

"I guess they leave them out here for when they have batting practice," said Mr. Jeter. "If you come out here when the team's not using the field, you can hit balls all afternoon. It's like having your own personal batting cage."

"My own personal ball field!" Derek said excitedly. "Dad, can we move here? Can we?"

"Whoa," Mr. Jeter said, holding up both hands and laughing. "We haven't even stepped inside the house yet."

"Who cares? We can fix it up if it's no good. Come on, Dad. Pleeeze?"

"Well, let's see if we can take a look first, okay?" Mr. Jeter replied as they crossed the street and went back to the car.

"It's a great location," Mr. Jeter told his wife. "And Derek *likes* it."

"Good. I'll write down the number and call the owner," said Mrs. Jeter. "What do you know?" she added in an amused tone. *"Derek likes it!"*

Chapter Fourteen

THE ROAD TO REDEMPTION

"For those of you who have become lazy and complacent with the arrival of warm weather," said Mr. Laithwaite, prowling the aisles of the classroom as his gaze darted from one student to the next, "let me remind you that your paper is due in exactly one week. It will count for a full one third of your social studies grade. So, I advise you to get busy. No less than six double-spaced pages—and don't just fill them with empty words, please. I hate empty words."

Derek got the message. But he had to think he was in good shape that way. His paper talked about a real issue, and it also had personal touches, stories of "addicts" he knew, and even his own sense of temptation. It was turning into a good paper, he felt sure.

Vijay, on the other hand, looked panicked, especially when Mr. L's eyes found him. Gary Parnell pretended to be taking notes, just so he wouldn't have to meet the teacher's gaze. Jeff Jacobson and Harry Hicks also looked guilty and uncomfortable, as did a few others in the class.

Derek wasn't sure about the others, but he would have bet they'd been spending their time at home on their video consoles, not playing sports as Gary Parnell would surely say in his paper on "sports addiction."

Derek could well understand the other kids' discomfort. He'd only been at the video game arcade that one day, and he'd gotten completely carried away. These kids, he knew for a fact, were there at least twice a week and sometimes more.

And every time Derek played at Vijay's house, he had a hard time tearing himself away from playing, even though he knew it was happening—knew in advance, even. He was sure he could have easily slipped into addiction over video games if he'd let himself.

Not that there was anything wrong with video games as such. They were creative, fun, and challenging, and many of them improved hand-eye coordination or were otherwise educational.

But as with anything else, you could have too much of a good thing. Medicine can become poison if you take too much of it, one of his aunts used to say.

Knowing where to draw the line was the key—so much,

and no more. It was hard, but that was the only way you could allow certain things into your life without them totally taking it over.

It had been a good assignment for the class, Derek decided. Everyone was going to learn something, one way or the other, either by succeeding or failing. He just hoped Vijay would get it together before next Monday.

On Friday afternoon the Jeter family got a chance to view the house on Cumberland Street behind the high school field.

Besides the basement level there were two floors. Upstairs there were three bedrooms and a bathroom. On the main floor was the living room, along with the kitchen and dining area. And in the basement, a big family room, along with an office for Mr. Jeter and an extra bathroom.

All in all, it wasn't anything spectacular. Sharlee wasn't thrilled, since she preferred both of the other houses to this one. But Derek didn't care if the house wasn't perfect. *Where it was* was perfect. As the agent had said, "Location, location, location!"

Derek searched his parents' faces for any sign of their thinking. They both seemed okay with the place, even if they weren't blown away by it.

"And you know, Derek," Mr. Jeter was saying, "it's only a ten-minute drive from Mount Royal."

"Cool," Derek said. "Can we rent it, Dad? Mom?"

"Well," said Mrs. Jeter, "what do you think, Charles?" It was rare for his mom to call his dad "Charles." Mostly she called him "Jeter."

"I like the office," he replied. "What do you think, Dot?"

"The layout works. And for Derek it's perfect."

Derek smiled, agreeing with her completely.

"What about me?" Sharlee complained. "Doesn't my opinion count?"

"Of course it does, honey," said Mr. Jeter. "But remember, you're going to be attending this high school too one day."

"Oh." Sharlee thought about that for a second. "Well, if we do move here, I want the big bedroom."

"Um, Sharlee, that's for me and your mom," said Mr. Jeter.

"Hey, that's okay," Derek said. "She can have the second-biggest. I'll take the small bedroom. I don't care."

"All right, then," said his mom. "I guess we can go for it. What do you say, Jeter?"

"Let's do it," he said.

Derek literally jumped for joy. Who would have ever thought he'd be this happy to move away from Mount Royal?

His parents called the owner as soon as they got home. They had to leave a message because no one picked up the phone.

"Okay, that's that," said Mrs. Jeter. "Now we just have to cross our fingers it isn't already rented."

After dinner Derek went back to work on his paper. He wanted to finish it that night because he had another doubleheader tomorrow and he didn't want to leave it for Sunday, the last day before the paper was due. So, he got permission from his parents to stay up late working on it.

By ten p.m. he was done and had gone over it three times for last-minute changes and corrections. He was satisfied that he'd done the best he could. Anyway, he was too tired to go any further. He put the paper into his book bag and got ready for bed. He'd sleep well tonight, he was sure. He wondered if Vijay was still up working.

It would be good to play ball with the Reds again. They'd lost another game without him on Wednesday, while he'd been at travel team practice. He'd been torn about that choice, as he had been all season. But in the end, being on the travel team was much more important to him. Playing against better competition was the only way he could improve his game and get to the next level. He laughed at himself.

"Sounds like I'm playing a video game," he muttered as he drifted off to sleep.

His teammates were glad to see him, even if they had noticed his absence. "Hey, the Phantom is back," Charlie joked.

Elliott borrowed someone else's cap, put it over his own cap but facing backward, and kept spinning around, saying, "I'm a Red. I'm a West-Sider. I'm a Red. I'm a West-Sider. . . ."

Even Derek had to laugh, because he could see they were more happy to see him than they were mad at him. And once the game started, they quickly forgot he'd ever been gone.

Derek hit cleanup and drove in two runs in the first inning. Then he held down the fort at shortstop, fielding two difficult hops in the first two innings.

By the top of the third, the Reds were up 3–0 and looking for more. Derek came to the plate for the second time, feeling more confident than he had since he'd gone into that horrendous slump.

This time, as if to bury the memory of the slump altogether, he hit a line drive that went all the way to the outfield fence, driving in two more runs. After a long slump, getting four RBIs in two at bats felt fantastic!

Yes, he was back to being his old self again, no doubt about it. Maybe it was getting the term paper done, maybe it was finding the perfect house to move to—or maybe even getting over his initial fascination with video games and back to concentrating on baseball.

For whatever combination of reasons, his normal confidence had resurfaced. "Oh yeah," he said under his breath as he stood on second base. "The kid is back in the groove!"

The Reds scored two more that inning, and although their opponents put together three runs in the fourth, they never really got back into it. Derek and his buddies wound up with an 11–4 victory, capped by his grand slam in the top of the fifth. That gave him a grand total of eight runs batted in, in just one game—his best hitting performance ever!

Now for the main event, he told himself as he packed up his gear after the game. This afternoon the West Siders would be playing the Cardinals. The two teams were tied for second place. They needed a win to keep up with the undefeated Mets, whom they would play the following week.

Derek only hoped his hitting groove would stay with him and not go missing for the big game.

Don't think about that, Derek told himself sternly. *That is not going to happen. No way.*

The West Siders were 3–1 so far this spring season. So were the Cardinals. The winner of this game would go to 4–1, the loser to 3–2. Meanwhile the undefeated Mets were playing the 1–3 Rangers. Even if they lost, the Mets would hold a share of first place.

"Derek," said Coach Russell, "you been working on that swing?"

"I have, Coach."

"Good. I liked what I saw last game. You're close, I can see that. So . . . you're leading off today, okay?"

"Me? Sure!" Derek hadn't led off all season, but hey, why not? He liked leading off. It made him more selective at the plate, which meant he got to see more pitches and get used to what was being thrown at him. It also let his teammates get a long look at the pitcher's stuff.

Another thing Derek liked about hitting leadoff was that it allowed him to focus on one thing only—getting himself on base, by whatever means necessary.

There was a big crowd today, and that was something else Derek always liked. For him playing ball was a performance, and the bigger the audience, the easier it was for him to rise to the occasion.

His whole family was there because Sharlee's game had ended before lunch. Her team had won again (they were still undefeated), and she'd kept on bragging about it all through lunch.

Well, that was fine with him. She had a lot to be proud of. Leading her league in home runs *and* batting average was not nothing, even if she was only seven years old.

Derek pointed over at his family, and they waved back. "This one's for you, Sharlee," he muttered under his breath. "Just to show you you're not the only good ballplayer in the family."

He stepped up to the plate and took the first two pitches, one for a ball and the other for a strike. Now he'd seen both a fastball and a changeup. *The next fastball I get, I'll be ready,* he thought.

After taking a curveball for ball two, he saw the fastball coming at him, high and over the plate. Back in the cages with his dad, he had practiced staying back and not lunging forward at the ball, trusting his hands to catch up to the pitch. And now he put his practice to the test.

THWACK! The screaming line drive made the second baseman duck for cover, and by the time the outfielders got near it, it was already past them, rolling all the way to the fence. Derek wound up with a triple to start the game.

Mason had no trouble driving him in, and Nate followed with a double to score the West Siders' second run. Harry walked, and after Mo and Brad struck out, Daxon singled to drive in the third run. Christian then grounded out to end the frame, but it was 3–0, West Siders, and the Cardinals hadn't even come to bat yet.

Harry had not been focused on baseball lately, and Derek knew why. He wondered where Harry got the money to hit the arcade so often. Maybe his parents were giving him too much allowance or something. Anyway, it was all getting fed into the coin slots at the arcade, not into a piggy bank.

And Harry's pitching had suffered with the lack of focus. His control was gone, and his fastballs were missing the plate.

He walked the first three hitters and only settled down after Coach Russell made an emergency mound visit. Harry then got two grounders and a strikeout, but two runs scored in the process and it was back to being a close game, at 3–2.

Another great thing about hitting leadoff, Derek

reflected, was that you got more at bats than anyone else on the team. Following a walk by Landon, Derek came to the plate for the second time, and it was only the second inning.

Derek let the first two pitches go by for strikes, hoping Landon would take the opportunity to steal second. When the third pitch got by the catcher, Landon did.

Now, with a runner in scoring position, Derek had an RBI opportunity. But with two strikes he had to protect the plate, too. He fouled off the next four pitches just to stay alive, even though a couple were probably off the plate. Then he got the pitch he wanted, a changeup.

Derek waited on it, then smacked it the other way. Landon was off like a rocket, and Derek took second on the late throw to the plate. Now it was 4–2, West Siders, and still nobody out.

Mason flied out to right, and Derek tagged up and went to third. But then Nate popped out to short for the second out.

"Come on, Harry," Derek shouted to his old friend. "Drive me in."

Harry nodded. But unlike Derek, he hadn't been practicing, and it showed. His swings were wild and out of control, and he struck out on three straight pitches, leaving Derek stranded on third base.

As Derek went to the bench and grabbed his mitt, he thought about all the times his parents had told him, "If you want to be a big-league ballplayer, you're going to have to outwork everyone else."

Well, Derek had mostly done that, with a few small exceptions. And all that hard work was starting to pay off.

Harry had always wanted to be a big leaguer too. But maybe he didn't want it as badly as Derek did. Or maybe he was so hooked on video games that he'd lost his focus and ambition.

Back at short Derek was soon tested. Harry was getting the ball over the plate now, but the Cardinals were hammering him. The first man doubled to the fence in center. The next guy hit a screamer that Derek had to dive full-out for. He grabbed it, and the crowd gasped and applauded. He was glad so many people were there to see him do it.

It got even better when the next hitter blooped one into foul territory behind third base. Derek and Brad both went for it, but Derek had the better angle. He called Brad off, then dived again—and caught it just before it hit the ground!

He could feel the burn as he slid across the grass. That was going to sting for a few days, for sure. But it had been well worth it.

Harry raised his hands over his head and clapped for Derek, and Derek pointed back at him, shouting, "Let's go!"

Seemingly inspired, Harry struck out the next hitter on three straight fastballs, to end the inning with the score still 4–2 in their favor.

The West Siders put two men on in their half of the third

but didn't score. Neither did the Cardinals in their half, as Harry settled down and put them away one, two, three.

Derek led off again in the fourth. This time he didn't see any pitches to his liking and worked a walk after getting the count to 3–2.

Mason followed with a long fly to center that was caught, on a good play right in front of the fence. Nate then singled Derek over to third, and after Harry struck out again, Mo came through with the big hit—a double that scored both runners!

Brad grounded out to end the frame, but now the West Siders' lead was 6–2.

Then Harry fell apart. He walked two men, got lucky on a great pick of a grounder by Derek, who threw to third to get the lead runner, then hit a batter to load the bases.

When Harry walked the next man to force a run in, Coach Russell made a change, bringing Mo in from second base to pitch, with Harry going to third and Brad to second.

Mo struck out the next two men, and everyone on the West Siders breathed a sigh of relief. They still had a three-run lead at 6–3, with only two innings to go.

The West Siders went down in order in the fifth, and Derek was stranded in the on-deck circle. *Oh well,* he thought. In the next inning he'd be leading off again. . . .

Mo got through the fifth without any damage, even though he gave up a double and a walk along the way.

Things were looking bright for the West Siders as Derek

stepped to the plate for his fourth at bat of the game. This time, with a three-run lead and only one inning left, he felt he could go for broke at the plate and try to put this game out of reach.

The Cardinals had seen Derek hold off on the first pitch every time so far. This time Derek was ready to swing at the first pitch he liked. It was a fastball right down the middle, and Derek didn't miss it.

The left fielder tried to run down the long fly, but it was just out of his reach. Derek pulled into second base easily, clapping his hands in excitement. "Come on!" he yelled, urging Mason on.

Mason put the ball in play, hitting a grounder to first that allowed Derek to advance to third. Then with one out Nate singled Derek home, for the team's seventh run!

The next two hitters struck out, but now they had a four-run lead. And Mo struck out the first two batters before getting the third to fly out to short. Derek cradled the ball in his mitt as he yelled, "YEAH!" and leapt into the air triumphantly.

The final score was 7–3, West Siders. They were alone in second place, and if the Mets lost later today, they'd be tied for first!

Derek hugged his teammates one after the other, then went over and found his family.

"Great game, Derek," his father shouted happily. "Some great swings today. You look like yourself again."

Derek was fairly bursting with happiness, having had his best game of the year, and one of his best ever.

But things got even better a few minutes later, when Coach Russell approached him, along with another man Derek didn't recognize.

"Great game, Derek," the coach told him, shaking hands and patting him on the cap.

"Thanks, Coach!" Derek said, hoping he wasn't blushing or sounding too conceited.

"That's a great swing you've got there, kid," said the other man.

"Derek, this is Mike Hinga," said Coach Russell. "He's the coach of the fourteen-and-up travel team."

"Oh! Wow!" Derek said, suddenly realizing the importance of what was going on. "Thank you, sir."

"No, thank *you*," said Coach Hinga. "You put on quite a show today, young man. Coach Russell told me to come down today and give you a look-see. I think I might have been watching our team's next shortstop."

"Wha—do you *mean it*?" Derek gasped, having a hard time believing his ears.

"Well, we'll see who else shows up to try out," Coach Hinga said. "But that was really impressive. I can't see you not making the team."

"Thanks!" Derek said breathlessly. "Um, but I won't be in fourteen-and-up for another year."

"Well, our shortstop's not moving on till then, so that

times out pretty nicely." He shook Derek's hand again. "Keep working on your game, kid," he said. "I'll have my eye on you in the meantime. And don't worry. If you stay with it, I'm pretty certain there'll be a place for you on the team when the time comes, one way or another."

It was a déjà vu moment for Derek. It was almost the same thing that had happened to him when Coach Russell had seen him at a Little League game and told him to try out for travel team.

It was like living a fairy tale—first travel team, now the fourteen-and-uppers . . .

Could it really end with his ultimate dream coming true?

Chapter Sixteen

FACING THE MUSIC

Derek had never been to a funeral, but the afternoon Mr. Laithwaite gave them back their papers, the mood in the classroom made him think of one.

When the bell rang to signal the end of the school day, no one spoke above a murmur. They just tucked their graded papers into their book bags and shuffled out into the hallway.

Derek himself wasn't feeling too bad. Mr. Laithwaite had given him an A-minus, praising Derek's diligent work and all the personal touches he'd added to make it real for the reader. He also complimented Derek's insights about his own flirtation with video game addiction.

Derek felt he'd earned his A-minus, and although he

would rather have gotten an A, he knew Mr. Laithwaite was a notoriously tough grader. The only negative comment was that he could have picked a more deadly addiction, given the perils that teens and even preteens faced from actual drugs and alcohol.

Derek had to shake his head about that one. When he'd given out the assignment, Mr. Laithwaite had taken pains to let them know there were many other addictions they could write about, besides drugs and alcohol. And now he was penalizing Derek for taking him up on it!

Still, an A-minus isn't exactly chopped liver, Derek told himself. *I wonder what grades all the other kids got.*

He found Vijay leaning against his locker, staring blankly into space. "My parents are going to take away my video games for sure when they find out I got a C-plus," he told Derek. "What am I going to do?"

Derek didn't know what to say. Several times in the past month, he'd reminded his usually diligent friend to get on with it and start his paper.

But Vijay had resisted writing it at every turn, preferring to bury himself in virtual worlds. Now the real world was biting back, with a vengeance.

"Aw, it's okay, Vij," Derek said, trying to comfort him. "You didn't get a failing grade. It could have been worse." But he knew that for a kid like Vijay, who almost always got As, a C-plus was a *major disaster*.

"It counts for a third of our grade!" he moaned, putting both hands on his head. "I'm busted. I won't see my video game system again for at least a year—maybe *forever*!"

"I'm sure your mom and dad won't take it away for *that* long," Derek said, although he really had no idea how they would react. "Anyway, you could probably use a little break from video games, right?"

Vijay shook his head slowly. "It's a disaster," he said. "Why didn't I work harder on that paper?"

Derek didn't know what to say. "Hey, you want to play some catch out on the Hill later?" he finally managed.

Vijay let out a humorless laugh. "Maybe," he said. "If they even let me. But either way, I'm going to be so bored without . . ." He broke off without finishing, but Derek could fill in the blanks.

"Hey, see you on the bus," he told Vijay, and left him there to pull himself together as best he could.

Would Vijay's parents really take away his console? Derek wondered. *Probably,* he thought. If it had been *his* parents, they would have *definitely* confiscated it, and for a good long time too.

Next Derek ran into Gary Parnell, who was more angry than devastated. "An A-*minus*?" he kept repeating in disbelief to whoever would listen. "This is so unfair!"

"What happened, Gary?" Derek asked him. "Didn't get your usual A-plus?" He was being provocative, and he knew it. But he and Gary had been going at each other forever over who could get the best grades, and usually Gary came out on top.

Not this time. "I got an A-minus too," Derek told him.

"For what? For writing about *video games*? Are you for real?"

"Hey, it's a real addiction," Derek shot back.

"Not like addiction to *sports*," Gary insisted. "Mr. Laithwaite must be a secret sports fan. His big complaint was that I should have chosen a more serious addiction. Can you believe it?"

Derek could certainly believe it. But he was in no mood to argue with Gary.

Derek himself was satisfied with his A-minus. Gary felt that his was a gross injustice and not worthy of the world-class paper he had submitted.

Well, that was Gary, and it probably always would be, Derek reflected.

On the bus he ran into Jeff and Harry, who were sitting next to each other, looking stunned. "What'd you guys get?" Derek asked them.

"C," said Harry.

"C-minus," said Jeff.

"Oh. Sorry, man. That stinks."

"What'd you get?" Harry asked him.

"Um . . . A-minus?"

"A-minus?" they both repeated.

"What'd you do to get that good a mark?" Harry wondered.

Derek shrugged. "I guess I just worked really hard on

it. I had good examples, too." He didn't mention that they were two of his prime examples.

Well, he thought as he took a seat across the aisle from them, *hopefully they'll realize that they have a problem and cut back on their video gaming.*

He had his doubts, though. Addictions were tough things to kick. That was one of the major lessons he'd learned from writing his paper.

He realized he'd been lucky not to get more deeply involved in video gaming. His passion for baseball had helped him keep focused on what mattered and not be distracted by temptation.

He sat back, waiting for the stragglers to board the bus. Here came Vijay, still looking devastated. Here came Gary, talking Vijay's ear off about the injustice of it all.

Derek closed his eyes and let out a deep breath. He felt bad for Vijay, but as for himself, he was pleased with the way things were shaping up.

He'd enjoyed his time in Little League so far, even though the Reds were not going to make the playoffs, and even though he'd only made it to a few of their games. His travel team was about to play for first place. And best of all, the fourteen-and-up coach had pretty much told him he could make the team!

All in all, Derek felt that his ultimate goal of playing shortstop for the New York Yankees was becoming more and more real with every passing year. He was sure it was possible, if only he kept working hard enough and never let up.

Now, if only the owner of that house would rent it to them, he'd have a real ball field right next to his backyard. He could see himself on a faster track to the big leagues if he had twenty-four-hour access to that field, instead of just relying on pickup games on Jeter's Hill. He could imagine himself getting into pickup games with the high schoolers, even as soon as this summer.

But would the house's owner rent it to them? It had been over a week now, with other people wanting to rent it and the owner not making up his mind.

Derek was keeping his fingers crossed that they got the place. It was amazing to him that he'd ever been against the idea of moving. But then, he'd never imagined getting his own baseball field in the bargain.

"Okay, we know the Mets are 5–0," said Coach Russell. "They're a perennial statewide powerhouse. They haven't even had a close game all season. But *that* . . ." He looked around at his team, meeting every kid's gaze one by one. "*That* is because they haven't played *us* yet!"

That brought a cheer from the assembled West Siders.

"Now, we're a better team than we were at the start of the season," he went on. "And that's because we've worked hard, we've learned from our mistakes, and we've been challenged every step of the way. The harder the challenge the better we've responded."

Again he sought out each of their gazes before continuing. "Today is going to be our biggest challenge yet. But we've got a secret weapon—we know what we're up against. The Mets? They have no idea. So let's show 'em, huh?"

"YEAH!" everyone shouted in unison.

"Come on, West Siders, let's do this thing," he finished, and everyone high-fived one another.

Harry, as usual, was their starting pitcher. Before the game Derek approached him to see how he was doing. "I'm banned from video games for the rest of the school year," he told Derek.

"Well," said Derek, "that's only two weeks. Not so terrible."

"Ugh," Harry responded. Obviously, to him it was *totally* terrible.

But now, on the mound, he seemed to have shucked off all the distractions of the past. From the start he was throwing darts, hitting his spots, and fooling the Mets' hitters. They managed only a single that first inning, and Derek helped wipe that runner out by making a great tag on an attempted stolen base.

On the other hand, the Mets' pitcher was a true fireballer. "Everybody gear up," Mason told them after he struck out leading off. "This guy's got some kind of heat!"

Derek was hitting second today. From the first pitch, a sizzling strike, he knew the West Siders would not be getting a ton of hits today. Instead he fouled off pitch after pitch, trying to work the kid's pitch count up and get him out of the game early.

After nine pitches Derek finally got a well-earned walk. He stole second as Nate took a strike, then hustled to third on a pitch that got away from the catcher.

Nate struck out, but Harry managed a dribbler down the third-base line. Derek had been running on contact with two outs. He crossed the plate just as Harry beat out the throw to first. 1–0, West Siders!

The Mets looked surprised, and then angry. They weren't used to playing from behind. When the next pitch hit Mo on the shoulder, angry words were exchanged between the teams.

The West Siders crowd, including Derek's family, was upset as well. It certainly looked like the Mets' pitcher had hit Mo on purpose.

Brad struck out to end the inning, so no further damage was done. But a lead was a lead, as long as they could defend it.

With one out in the top of the second, the Mets' hitter doubled to right. Derek then saw that the kid was looking to steal third. So on the first pitch to the next hitter, Derek snuck in behind the runner, who was way off the bag. Landon fired a bullet of a throw right past Harry, who had to duck. The ball smacked into Derek's glove exactly where the runner's hand was reaching out for the bag as he dived. "OUT!" called the ump.

The West Siders and their fans cheered. Now the bases were empty with two out.

The next hitter drove one to center, but Mason ran it down and made a sparkling catch to save a possible home run.

It was still 1–0 when the West Siders came to bat in the bottom of the second. Daxon led off by laying down a bunt and beating it out for a single. Christian hit a pop-up behind second that somehow dropped in for a hit. Daxon, who'd been holding back in case the ball was caught, just made it to second, but now there was a rally brewing, with two on and nobody out.

Landon grounded out, but the runners both advanced. Mason then popped up to third for the second out, and up came Derek.

This guy throws so hard, I'm going to get my swing started early, he thought as he stepped into the box. He choked up a little on the bat and held his arms farther up and back than normal, to get off a quicker swing.

CRACK!

Derek's liner to left was the first hard-hit ball by the West Siders that day. It skidded past the outfielder and went all the way to the fence. Both runs scored, and Derek made it to third. The West Siders' bench was wild with excitement, and so were their fans.

"Go, Derek!" Sharlee yelled, her voice reaching him over the rest as it always did. He spotted her in the crowd and waved to her, then noticed that Coach Hinga was in the bleachers too.

Derek was thrilled that the coach had come back to watch them again, and even more thrilled that Derek had another chance to impress the man he hoped would be his coach next year. But there was no time to think about that now. Derek turned his attention back to business.

Nate swung through two strikes. *The pitcher's going to throw something off the plate next, hoping Nate will swing at a bad one,* Derek told himself, deciding to do something radical and shocking.

The pitch was a ball, and Derek took a big lead off third, provoking the catcher to run at him with the ball. When the catcher chased him back and threw to third, and the ball got past the third baseman. Derek quickly reversed course and ran home, scoring the West Siders' fourth run!

When Nate struck out on the next pitch, it almost didn't matter. The team was up 4–0, and the Mets' aura of invincibility was gone.

On defense the West Siders were playing like a finely tuned machine. Mason turned in two sparkling plays in the outfield that inning. And after the West Siders went down one, two, three in their half of the third, they snuffed out a Mets rally in the fourth, with Derek starting a nifty six-four-three double play.

The West Siders did manage only a walk in their half

of the fourth. The Mets were limited to a single in the top of the fifth.

Then, in the bottom of the fifth, the Mets put in a new pitcher. *Thank goodness,* thought Derek, who was about to lead off the inning.

Watching the new guy warm up, Derek felt distinctly less intimidated. This kid was not nearly as much of a fireballer as the Mets' starter.

Hunting a fastball, Derek pulled the first strike he saw into left field, starting the inning off with a double. Nate then singled him home, before the next three West Siders went down in order.

But it was 5–0 now, and the mighty Mets were down to their last licks!

Mo was pitching, and when the leadoff man bunted for a single, it seemed to rattle him. He walked the next two batters to load the bases with no one out, and the Mets were clearly smelling blood in the water.

Derek hunkered down at short. *Hit it to me,* he begged silently. *Hit it right here.*

SMACK! A screaming line drive soared above Derek's head. He leapt, stuck out his glove, and snagged it, then turned without even a glance and fired to second to catch the runner off base for a double play!

The Mets did score a run when the next hitter singled. But Mo buckled down and struck out the next guy to end the game—5–1, West Siders, in a mega-upset shocker!

The West Siders' fans exploded in joy, and the players kept hugging one another, tossing their mitts into the air and hurling themselves into a joyous pile of players.

They'd done it. They were 5–1, just like the Mets—but because they'd *beaten* them head-to-head, the West Siders were now in first place!

Derek felt happy right down to his shoes. The team was riding high, and he'd been a huge part of it!

On June 26 the Jeter family held a quiet celebration at home. There was so much to celebrate.

The end of the school year and the start of summer, for one thing. Then there were the trophies. Sharlee had an MVP plaque from her team to go with a championship trophy. Meanwhile, Derek's travel team was in first place, and Derek had high hopes that another piece of shiny hardware would soon be standing on the table next to Sharlee's.

True, Derek's Little League team had come in dead last. He'd told his family about feeling like he'd let the team down. But his mom and dad had both assured him that he'd done everything he could to help them win.

"You set your priorities, and you stuck by them," his mom pointed out.

In fact, they'd won all three games he'd showed up at—and lost every one he'd missed. It pained Derek a little—but only a little. Because on top of everything else they were celebrating, today was Derek's thirteenth birthday!

"You made it, old man!" said his mom, kissing him on the cheek as he blew out the candles on the cake she and Sharlee had made him. It had three tiers and was shaped like Yankee Stadium. Derek hated to cut into it, but after a few pictures, it was too hard to resist.

"Yum!" he said between mouthfuls. "Great job on this cake, you guys! Mmm!"

"Do you feel any different now that you're a teenager?" Sharlee asked him.

Derek thought about it. "Not really . . . but kind of . . ."

"Well, that explains everything," said Sharlee sarcastically.

"Seriously, it's hard to explain," he said. "Something's different. . . . I just don't know what it is yet."

And probably the biggest thing to celebrate (as if all that weren't enough) was that the family would be moving to their new house in September! After haggling with his parents for over three weeks, the owner had finally called that very morning and agreed to give them a two-year lease.

"Remember, you promised me the bigger bedroom," Sharlee reminded Derek.

"I know, I know," Derek said. "Boy, that was a dumb move on my part."

"Too bad, so sad," Sharlee said, with a grin that made Derek burst out laughing.

Just then the phone rang. Derek went to get it. "Hello?"

"Happy Birthday, Derek!" It was Vijay. "What's happening over there?"

"Oh, hey! We were just having some cake."

"Mmm. Save me a piece, okay? Listen, what're you up to later?"

"Nothing much. Why?"

"Do you want to meet up on the Hill and play some catch?"

Derek guessed Vijay's parents had, indeed, taken away his video game console. "Sure, man. Meet you in half an hour?"

"Cool! See you there."

Derek hung up and sat back down to finish his cake. He felt deeply happy and satisfied. The summer lay ahead, filled with visits to New Jersey, travel baseball games, and fun with friends and family.

And when summer was over, he'd be living in their new house—with a baseball field right behind it! Next year, he would almost surely be on the fourteen-and-up travel team. *And*, the year after that, he might be wearing the maroon-and-white uniform of the Kalamazoo Central High School Giants!

Derek cut himself another piece of cake, because a moment like this was too good to let go of without a second helping. The future was looking brighter and brighter.

Challenge met, he said to himself. *Now bring on the next one!*

REDS' LITTLE LEAGUE ROSTER:

George Eng, CF

Charlie Morgenstern, 3B, P

Zeke Martin, P, 3B

Derek Jeter, SS

Ernesto Alvarez, C

Elliott Koppel, RF

Norman Nelson, LF

Ben Tabor, 1B

Matt Lowe, 2B

WEST SIDERS' TRAVEL TEAM ROSTER:

Mason Adams, CF

Nate Wallace, 2B, SS

Derek Jeter, SS, LF, 1B

Harry Hicks, P, 3B, 1B

Mo Salem, 1B, P, 3B

Brad Russell, 3B

Daxon Parker, LF

Christian Parker, RF

Landon August, C

(Eli Warren, alternate)

JETER PUBLISHING

Jeter Publishing's tenth middle-grade book is inspired by the childhood of Derek Jeter, who grew up playing baseball. The middle-grade series is based on the principles of Jeter's Turn 2 Foundation.

Jeter Publishing encompasses adult nonfiction, children's picture books, middle-grade fiction, ready-to-read children's books, and children's nonfiction.

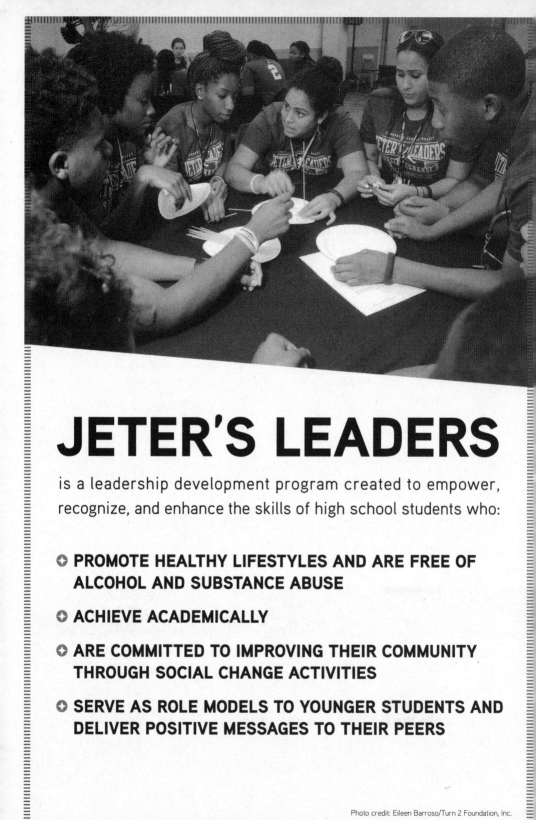

JETER'S LEADERS

is a leadership development program created to empower, recognize, and enhance the skills of high school students who:

- ➤ **PROMOTE HEALTHY LIFESTYLES AND ARE FREE OF ALCOHOL AND SUBSTANCE ABUSE**

- ➤ **ACHIEVE ACADEMICALLY**

- ➤ **ARE COMMITTED TO IMPROVING THEIR COMMUNITY THROUGH SOCIAL CHANGE ACTIVITIES**

- ➤ **SERVE AS ROLE MODELS TO YOUNGER STUDENTS AND DELIVER POSITIVE MESSAGES TO THEIR PEERS**